MOTHERS OF THE DISAPPEARED

*Dundee-based private investigator
J. McNee finds his past is about to catch
up with him in this intriguing mystery.*

When the mother of a murdered child asks
PI J McNee to re-open a case he helped
close during his time in the police, McNee is
faced with some uncomfortable questions. Is
the wrong man serving a life sentence for a
series of brutal murders? If so, why did he
admit his guilt before the court? McNee
must make a terrifying moral choice.

* *available from Severn House*

MOTHERS OF THE DISAPPEARED

A J. McNee Mystery

Russel D. McLean

Severn House Large Print
London & New York

This first large print edition published 2015
in Great Britain and the USA by
SEVERN HOUSE PUBLISHERS LTD of
19 Cedar Road, Sutton, Surrey, England, SM2 5DA.
First world regular print edition published 2014 by
Severn House Publishers Ltd., London and New York.

British Library Cataloguing in Publication Data

McLean, Russel D. author.
  Mothers of the disappeared.
  1. McNee, J. (Fictitious character)--Fiction. 2. Dundee
  (Scotland)--Fiction. 3. Detective and mystery stories.
  4. Large type books.
  I. Title
  823.9'2-dc23

  ISBN-13: 9780727897701

Severn House Publishers support the Forest Stewardship Council™
[FSC™], the leading international forest certification organisation. All
our titles that are printed on FSC certified paper carry the FSC logo.

Printed and bound in Great Britain by
T J International, Padstow, Cornwall.

For Lesley
Literary Critic. Doctor of Joyce.
Drinker of Prosecco.
With love.
(And wine)
(And chocolate)

2011

'Five years,' the old bugger says. 'Five years since I offered you the chance to come and work with me.'

'Aye,' I say, 'and I'm here now.' Playing it cool. This is how it is. Neither of us can change anything.

He's not buying it. Why would he? This isn't the usual dance. We're learning new moves here, and he's not convinced about the tempo.

'Things have changed, then? The events of the last few weeks, perhaps?'

'A lot of things changed,' I say. 'But the last two years ... Maybe I made a few wrong choices.'

He nods. 'I understand. You've lost a lot. Your friends. Your woman. Your reputation. And now ... you understand ... don't you? Finally.'

He sees the way his words sting. But he doesn't gloat. We're walking a fine line here. Like close friends tipping over into lovers; one wrong move and everything we've worked towards is irrevocably destroyed.

The simile, of course, is a little on the nose.

'You need to prove to me that you're serious.'

7

He talks slowly. Calmly. His eyes refuse to leave mine. Searching for any sign of deception.

I meet his gaze. 'What do you need?'

'Information. That's all. You can get me some information, can't you? Isn't that what you do for people all the time?'

'I guess so. What kind of information?'

He leans forward. 'Are you an artistic man, Mr McNee? Do you like taking photographs?'

'Can't say it's a passionate hobby.' I always said I'd never stoop to the peeping Tom jobs. But that was another time. Another life. Before everything changed.

He nods. 'Just need you to watch an address for me. A hotel room.'

He waits for a moment. Perhaps thinking I'll ask for more detail. This is all part of the test. He needs to know how many of my principles I'm willing to abandon for him.

After he's sure I'm not going to say anything, he writes down an address for me. Passes the scrap of paper across the desk. I read it, try not to smile.

He knows what he's doing, the wily old shite-bag. He's been waiting for this moment.

Who can blame him?

This is his tipping point. This is the moment when he finally owns me.

He's always talked like I'm the son he never had. Truth is, he just wants power over me. Same as with everyone he meets. David Burns wants you to know that he's the man in charge. That he owns you. Owns everyone you know.

'Well?' he says.

I don't hesitate this time. 'Long as you pay up front.'

Can he see what I'm really feeling?

'Is cash acceptable?'

'Sure,' I say. 'For a job like this.'

I stand and offer my hand. He stands, too, and when we shake, he continues to lock his eyes on to mine.

When I leave the room, I feel different.

Like someone just paid for my soul.

ONE

I stared at the letter.
  Read it again.
  Again.

Dear Mr McNee
  In light of recent charges brought against your
agency, the Association of British Investigators
has been forced to consider your current active
status. Until such time as a full investigation can
be conducted, your membership will be suspend-
ed...

I placed the letter back on the desk, stood
up, crossed the floor of the office to the window. Looked out across to the DSS building,
beyond to the rear of the Overgate Shopping
Centre. Sandstone and steel, a far cry from
its heyday as a concrete monstrosity inflicted
on the city during the sixties, when the
council had proceeded to destroy any vestige
of character the city may have possessed. It
had long been a symbol of the new Dundee;
a city looking to the future rather than re-
membering its past.

11

I sucked in a heavy breath, let it go. Slow. Like a smoker's last desperate gasp on his final fag-end.

The word *suspended* echoed in my head.

Someone laughed.

Of course, it took a moment before I realized it was me.

I called on Lindsay. At his house.

Bad idea?

Maybe. But things had changed between us since he came out of the coma. We weren't friends. Never would be. But we'd found an uneasy alliance in shared experience.

And shared betrayal.

As always, answering the door, he didn't smile. Didn't say anything. Just stepped back to allow me inside.

Maybe twenty seconds before his opening gambit: 'How long did it take you to put away the crutches?'

'I still have them,' I said. 'Just in case.'

Five years earlier, I'd been involved in a car accident. Wound up with a limp that the doctors said had no real physical cause.

These days, I limped less. And life was good. So go figure if there was a connection.

We went through to the sitting room, Lindsay taking the lead, his gait awkward, cane tap-tapping an off-beat rhythm on the hardwood floors.

The TV was on BBC daytime; middle-class timewasters searching for bargains at a car-boot sale. Lindsay said, 'Better than morphine.'

Sure, and without the entertainment value.

It was strange, not to hear him swear. Like he was the same man, but not quite. Until recently, I'd known next to nothing about who DCI George Lindsay was off the job.

He had a six-year-old son, and didn't want the lad to grow up hearing daddy swear.

Double standards?

We all have them. And if you can't swear when you're overseeing a brutal murder investigation, then God only knows when you can.

Lindsay and I sat across from each other. I took the sofa. He took a faux-leather armchair. Manoeuvred down awkwardly. The plastic leather creaked.

I pretended not to notice. 'Have you heard from her?'

He shook his head. 'Thought she'd contact you. You know. Considering.'

'Nothing since she left.'

Susan and I had a strange relationship, made worse when she lied to protect a teenage girl who murdered a man – a monster – in self-defence. The secret had brought us together before it eventually pushed us further apart than we had ever been.

There was a physics lesson in there, I was

sure of that.

Susan decided to go travelling. Told me she wanted to 'find herself'.

I didn't know what it meant then, and over six months later I wasn't any more clued-in. Except that whatever she was doing, she wasn't saying much about it beyond the occasional postcard and awkward email.

Now the only person I had left to talk to was Lindsay.

Aye, well, laugh it up. We were, after all, the best of enemies. Even when we'd been on the force, the antagonism had got the better of our professional instincts more than once.

But then he took a beating while trying to help me uncover the truth behind the death of Susan's father. The attack severe enough to put him in a coma. During those weeks, the ones that turned into months before he finally decided to come back to the world, I found myself in the habit of visiting his bedside and unburdening myself.

A confessional without the religious trappings.

I wonder if he heard me during those weeks. Since he woke up, neither of us have talked about it. But something had definitely changed between us.

Why I found myself in his front room at half nine on a Tuesday morning.

I told him about the letter. About the reason it had been sent.

14

'You shouldn't be talking to me about that.'

'Why not?'

He didn't say anything. I took his meaning. This was trouble coming home to roost. Maybe for both of us.

Four years earlier, I had killed a man. Shot him in the chest one rainy night in the centre of the Necropolis graveyard out to the west end of the city.

Self-defence.

The man had been a killer himself. Two days earlier he had killed a woman on the run from her gangster husband. And that evening, he'd been looking to take me out.

I always wondered whether Lindsay – the investigating officer on the case – truly believed the story I sold him, or if he had chosen to fudge the details for his own inscrutable reasons, letting me off the hook, justifying my actions on that rain-soaked evening.

Four years later, someone was raising doubts as to the official account of what happened. Questioning not just my story but the investigation into the events.

It wasn't Lindsay. He'd be throwing away his own reputation if he raised questions about that night. Besides, if he'd wanted to lock me up and throw away the key, he'd have done it there and then. Maybe things would have been better if he had.

We were quiet for a while. Lindsay was the one who broke the silence, asking, 'So what are you going to do?'

'Nothing I can do.'

'Really?'

'Except wait.'

He nodded. 'Welcome to my world.'

He was awaiting the results of a physical. Nearly eleven months of leave, he wanted back on the job, even if he was just driving a desk. But they were making him jump through hoops. Almost literally. Police work requires a certain degree of fitness, and given what happened to him, no one was sure that he would ever return to that level. He hated the tests, and even worse hated the possibility that he might not be allowed back.

I'd joked that he could go private. He'd almost knocked my block off.

We sat together for almost an hour, not saying much. Mostly exchanging half-hearted observations about the re-opening of the investigation and why anyone would start to look into it now. But neither of us had any answers, and the truth was that after four years we just wanted to forget it all, and move on with our lives.

I'd done enough standing still to last a lifetime.

When I got up to leave, he said, 'I stand by the report, you know. Back it all the way.'

I nodded to indicate that I understood.

And then I left.

About as close to friends as we could be.

I was suspended from the ABI, but the law didn't require that I shut down my business. The ABI has been working with the Government for years to legalize the profession, but the inevitable red tape has held up many attempts to organize our merry band into something approaching a cohesive professional body.

So I could work under the radar if I wanted. Say I was doing favours for friends. That kind of thing.

I had myself a part-time security gig with a bunch of other eyes from Fife, providing protection for a top-level golf tournament in St Andrews. Rich assholes, richer movie stars, tourists looking to get too close, as though the success might rub off on them.

I drove over the road bridge, slipped on sunglasses as the day brightened. It was the arse-end of summer, the weather unpredictable. For the best part of June and July the heat had been on, and even on dark days, you could see the red remnants of the Scottish suntan among the populace who'd taken advantage of the sun. We're pathetic that way. Scottish skin sizzles easy, and yet the first sign of a heatwave, we're out there, topless, not even bothering with the weakest of suncream.

Eejits.

I pulled up outside the Old Course Hotel, right next to Andy McDowell's gleaming BMW. He was leaning on the bonnet, waiting for me. Dressed all in black: a pasty Johnny Cash. Tipped his shades at me as I climbed out.

'We need to talk, McNee.'

'Something wrong?'

'I don't like to do this—'

I knew what he was going to say. Didn't let him finish, just raised a hand.

'Come on, man,' he said. 'Don't be like that.'

I'd worked with Andy on and off since I got into the investigation game. Originally from Glasgow, he formed McDowell Associates after moving to the east coast to indulge his passion for golf. He'd probably have preferred to move to Tennessee to indulge his passion for Americana, but sometimes in life you have to compromise. His connections to the golf world allowed him access to cake-walk security details like The Open. And he liked to work with people he knew.

He wouldn't take a decision like letting someone go without giving it a great deal of consideration. On all sides.

Didn't make me feel any better, though.

'I have policies,' he said. 'Everyone ABI certified and—'

'Do you believe I did it?'

'I don't know what you're supposed to have done,' he said. 'Just that you're off the register. But I'm sure that—'

'So what happens now?'

'There's a severance in the contract,' he said. 'You saw it. It's generous enough.' Aye, generous enough, he didn't mind being an arsehole.

'Doesn't really help.' It wasn't about the money. He knew that, probably understood. And all I was doing now was making this tough on him.

'Maybe you should take some time off while—'

'Would you?'

He didn't say anything.

I walked past him, stared out across the course and at the ocean. The wind was low, but you could still see the foam of breakers forming as the water lapped into the coastline.

'You want to talk about it?' he asked.

'Not really.'

'How about a beer?'

I looked at my watch. 'It's only just gone twelve.'

'Beer and lunch.'

'You've got work.'

'I've got people working.'

'Yeah,' I said. 'I was supposed to be one of them.' I moved back to the car, started to climb in.

Andy placed his hand on top of the open door before I had a chance to close it. 'If you were in trouble, you'd ask for help, right?'

I reached up and pushed his hand away before closing the door. He stayed where he was as I reversed, and then pulled out.

Looking in the rear-view, I saw him watch me. His shades hid what he was thinking.

But I could guess.

TWO

Back at the office, I stewed.

Windows closed. Door locked. In my chair, staring at piles of looming paperwork. Considering just chucking everything out of the window.

Maybe follow it all.

That last thought a joke.

Probably.

Dot buzzed through from the office. 'Someone to see you.'

'You know that I'm not currently taking—'

'Police.'

I stood up, unlocked the door, opened it. Sandy Griggs nodded at me in greeting. He was still tall and rangy, as I remembered. But his fine red hair was wispy, and you could see his scalp beneath strands that looked like they'd been styled by a gale-force wind. His blue suit fitted him a little awkwardly.

But the geek-edge of his appearance belied a quick and fiery anger that had occasionally taken him before Discipline and Complaints during his time with Tayside Police. Guess I could empathize with that. Especially given that the worst of his ire had been directed towards wife-beaters and domestic abusers. Some cops have their own personal agenda. Sandy always wore his on his sleeve. Why it was a surprise when he upped sticks to join the SCDEA, go hunt down the gangsters.

But those days were behind him. In an official capacity, at least.

Now Sandy was SCDEA.

Scottish Crime and Drug Enforcement Agency. Our very own Serious and Organized. Or, if you wanted to get all sound bite about it: the Scottish FBI.

Sandy stepped forward, one hand outstretched. I accepted the gesture, noted that he grasped just a little too long before letting go.

'Ja—' He caught himself, let his gaze drop for just a moment. Showing me he was embarrassed. Something told me it was a show. Work in the investigation game long enough, your shite detector gets a good workout. He was trying to show me that he remembered me well enough, that we were friends, even if we hadn't spoken in a long time. 'McNee. How you doing?'

'Good. Didn't think we'd see you round these parts any more. Thought you'd be too busy living the good life out on the west coast, keeping busy with the Glasgow gangs and all.'

'Aye, doesn't mean we're not watching over you guys here. Mind if we have a chat?' He didn't glance at Dot, but he might as well have done. 'In private?'

'I can close the door.'

He thought about that for a second. 'Fancy a coffee?'

Five minutes of sunshine in Dundee meant the pavement cafes were set up outside pubs and coffee houses in what was called, with some small sense of irony, the city's Cultural Quarter. Sandy took me to one of the busier set-ups, ordered for us.

I sat at the table with my sunglasses on and thought about what he might want to discuss.

Sandy had been a DI back in the day. Young, possibly ambitious, but occasionally scuppered by that anger. Hence his decision to change direction and work with the SCDEA. I'd been in uniform, then. Remembered his departure as abrupt, the change in direction no doubt something to do with the shitstorms he allowed himself to get into following a friendship with another private eye. I'd met the eye – his name was Bryson – only twice, but knew that he was the kind of man who got his friends into trouble whether he meant to do it or not. Bad news followed him around like a sulky Rottweiler.

No wonder Sandy was acting like he knew

me. I had more than a few things in common with his old friend.

When Sandy came back, he placed my coffee in front of me and kept a hold of his own mug as he sat down. 'Sorry to drag you away from your busy day.'

'Not a problem.'

We both sipped at our drinks. Keeping eye contact. Giving away as little as possible. Daring: call my bluff.

Around us, ordinary people indulged in ordinary conversations about kids, work, last night's TV.

Sandy didn't want to talk about any of that. Neither did I.

So he said, no pre-amble, 'That night, did you have another gun on your person?'

I started to get up. His hand shot out and grabbed my wrist. 'That's not why I'm asking.'

'All due respect, I think it is.'

Sandy let go of me. I sat down. Waited for an explanation. Ready to leave if I didn't like it.

'The reason I ask is that I want you to say you did. Even if it's not true.'

'You want my business to tank?'

He hesitated. 'You could say that,' he said. And told me why.

The man I killed – and I still can't say whether it was an accident, or in cold blood

24

– worked for London gangster Gordon Egg. Egg was old-school hard-arse, had been waging a war in Dundee against a man named David Burns. The dead man was one of Egg's best muscle-men.

I shouldn't have got involved, but a client was mixed up in their turf war, and I'd managed to get noticed by both sides. Burns, claiming to recognize something of himself in me, manipulated me, made sure I wound up doing his dirty work. I didn't agree to anything, but all the same found myself in the right place at the right time and with the proper motivation.

Since that night, Burns and I had what you might call a complicated relationship. He manipulated me again, forcing me into a hunt for his missing god-daughter, before using the death of an old friend to once more trick me into doing his dirty work. Looking at it from the outside, you might start to think I was enjoying it.

Which was precisely why Sandy Griggs wanted me to cosy up to the old man. To finally give in to everything he offered me. To quit being manipulated and willingly do exactly what the foosty old fuck wanted.

'You're a mental case,' I said. 'You know that, aye?'

He smiled. No humour. No warmth.

A couple took the table next to us. Oblivious to what was happening. Wrapped up in each other, laughing and sharing intimate little stories as they leaned in close across the table.

Wonder how me and Griggs would have appeared to them if they noticed us.

'Seriously. I can't do it.'

'Then what are you going to do?' Griggs asked. 'You're fucked, McNee. You know it. From the minute you made the decision to kill that man, you've been in freefall. The pavement's coming up fast. One way or another, it's going to hurt when you land.'

I massaged my forehead for a moment. Thinking about what he was asking me.

He leaned back, sipped at his coffee.

Sixteen months or so earlier, a good man had died because he lost track of what side of the law he was really on. Ernie Bright had been a good copper, and tried the trick of cosying up to the bad guys. It was a move that wound up killing him by inches until a shotgun blast to the chest finally put him out of his misery.

I still believed, even if others didn't, that Ernie hadn't switched sides. That he'd had some grander purpose. That he hadn't died uncertain of who he was, of who he stood for.

Sandy was asking me to walk that same line. More than that, he was asking me to betray every principle I had ever claimed to

26

have.

'I don't want to do this, man. But I'm down to my last hand. You're my ace.'

'Let me think about it. Jesus fuck, just give me a moment to...'

'Sure, a moment.' Griggs stood up. His coffee wasn't even half-finished. 'You know where I am. Just don't take too long, huh?'

THREE

I spent the afternoon making phone calls. Calling in what few favours I could. Shaking proverbial trees. Trying to get some idea of just how badly I was being fucked.

Nobody wanted to talk to me. Told me just about everything I needed to know.

Three o'clock got me a phone call from Cameron Connelly at the *Dundee Herald*. Playing the concern-for-a-friend card, but just beneath the genuine worry, I could hear his reporter's instincts angling for a story. If he was calling me, it meant his colleagues were already sniffing blood, and he wanted to beat them to the exclusive.

I said, 'How long?'

'They're waiting for official sources to disclose the nature of the charges.'

'How much do you know? Off the record, of course.'

'About what I knew before. Except the spin is different. Someone's trying to make this about your incompetence.'

'That how you'll report it?'

'I'll report the facts. You'll have right of

reply. But I don't want to run this if it's simply a vendetta, know what I'm saying?'

'You're all heart.'

'Aye, it's been said.'

In those days, I had been angry. Recovering – slowly – from the accident that had left me ready to lash out at the whole world. When I wound up caught in the middle of Burns's and Egg's little turf war, I focused my anger on two of Egg's thugs. Convinced there was no other option. Ask me today, I think things went the only way they could. Given who they were. Given who I was. Anyone trying to spin me as a have-a-go hero or a mindless thug was grinding their own axe.

The only witness to what happened that evening – the thug who survived – refused to talk to the police, to confirm or deny my story. Took the whole 'honour amongst crooks' bit dead serious. Dead being the operative word when he wound up knifed in prison just a few months later. The work of David Burns. He might as well have left his signature at the scene. But of course, even if everyone knew he had been behind the death, no one could prove it in a court of law.

So that left me. The only one who knew the truth. I had acted in self-defence. The gun was not mine.

So the questions became, *Why now?* Who was re-opening the investigation?

'Look, this just fell in my lap.'

'From where?'

'Talk.'

'Come on!'

Connelly sucked in a sharp breath on the other end of the line. 'Just talk, man. Words. Here and there. I know someone who's been hearing the whispers. What I can gather is that the word came in from an anonymous source. And given your recent relationship with the force, I guess they'd be more than inclined to look for ways to burn you.'

It was a fair point. I'd exposed one of their top cops as a corrupt arsehole playing both sides against the middle. I'd made enemies of the personal and political persuasions. And a number of coppers still thought I'd fitted up Kevin Wood. Refused to believe the evidence that their own Discipline and Complaints department had amassed against the deceased former deputy chief constable.

I wasn't about to get any answers from the force. And seeking answers from the ABI or any of my private contacts was a dead end. Connelly wasn't about to give me his source, and the way he told it, so far he was the only reporter aware of what was going on. This left my options limited. Giving me no choice but to go ask the questions I'd been too scared to ask earlier that day. Call in favours I'd never really earned.

30

'Don't start thinking we're going to become bosom buddies,' Lindsay said. 'Just because I have a modicum of gratitude for what you did...'

I still couldn't get used to it. When he was in the house, he didn't swear. His wife had tried to tell me as much when I met her in the hospital while the grumpy old bastard was in a coma, but I hadn't believed her.

'I need a favour.'

'Not much I can do moping around on the couch all day. Not much I'd want to do for you, anyway.' The barb was sluggish, more force of habit than genuine enthusiasm. You could see by the way he was sitting – back curved, head slumped just a little, arms hanging there – that he had lost something of the *joie de vivre* he once had. And who could blame him? Spend time in a coma, see how you feel when you come out of it. Especially when the people who put you there were people you were supposed to trust. Fellow police officers turned rent-a-thugs desperate to protect a powerful man's secrets.

I remember talking to Lindsay's wife after he came out of the coma. She told me that a little something inside him had died. That he wasn't quite the same man. Not just his quieter demeanour. There was the sense of shell-shock to him, as though his whole world had been turned upside down.

He hadn't been able to defend himself.

31

I think that was the worst thing for a man like Lindsay. He's always been proud. Used to take great pride in the fact that he was an outsider; granted grudging respect because of his by-the-book mentality, but never really one of the gang because of his refusal to form relationships within the job.

Then again, I'd taken the opposite tack, and look at which of us became the pariah.

'You're bored,' I said. 'I get that. When I took time off after the accident, all I wanted was get out there and do something. It drove me crazy.'

'Aye, turned you into a bigger arsehole than you already were.' Just a growl, a hint of the old bastard I used to know. Brought a smile to my face. Christ, times were bad when I got nostalgic for a man like George Lindsay.

'I'm not asking for much,' I said. 'Just a name. That's all.'

'And what happens when they ask me why I want to know?'

'You can work that out.'

'I just want to congratulate whoever stuck the knife in.'

'Always knew you had a sneaky side.'

He didn't say anything.

'Look, I just need to know,' I said. 'Something about the timing of all this seems very convenient.'

'Convenient, how?'

32

He couldn't work it out? I had to wonder if the coma had slowed him a touch more than anyone realized. 'I'll tell you if you get me the name.'

Another hesitation. I hoped he was thinking it over.

Persuasion is a delicate art. Like the police interview. You have to know when to push and when to step back. Go too much in either direction, you lose the control of the situation that you crave.

'I'll see what I can do,' he said. 'But that's it. Anyone wants to talk, I'll listen but there's no fu— no way, I'm putting my own reputation on the line for you. You go down, it's on your own. Right?'

'That's all I'm asking,' I said. 'That's all I'm asking.'

That evening, I stayed up late in the front room, sitting in the padded armchair, watching reruns on the TV. Most of them made little sense. TV scheduling goes out the window when you work my kind of gig, and with more and more TV built around story arcs and viewer loyalty, it meant that I just let the images wash over me.

In the end, I found that it wasn't enough of a distraction and turned off the set. I needed engagement. Something I could follow, could lose my brain in. I grabbed a book from the shelf – *American Skin*, by an Irish

writer Cameron Connelly had recommended to me a couple of months back – and
settled in.

I finished by 2 a.m., and the idea of coming back to reality made my stomach do
flips. I placed the book on the arm of the
chair, and closed my eyes, thinking I would-
n't sleep.

But I did.

My dreams were a mess of blood and fear.

It was the damn book that did it; a nightmare ride with a cast of psychopaths. Much
as I enjoyed it while awake, it came back to
haunt my subconscious.

Unlike the book, there was no narrative to
the dream. No way I could later describe it
other than as a dread feeling when I woke; a
half-memory of the dead.

They were all there.

The innocent.

The guilty.

All of them. People whose deaths I was
linked to, causally and explicitly.

They were there, in my dreams, watching
me, saying nothing. After all, there really was
nothing they could say.

FOUR

I was in the kitchen, making coffee. Trying to shake memories from my brain. The mobile buzzed its way across the counter. Gave me the salvation I'd been searching for. I grabbed it and answered.

'I have a name.'

'You're just going to give it to me?'

Lindsay tried his best not to sigh. 'You made a lot of enemies, the way you quit, you know that? Not just my friends, either.' I'd broken his nose the day I left the force. A flair for the dramatic? Or just a dickhead move? Used to be I thought I knew the answer, now I wasn't so sure. 'Never mind some of the crap you pulled over the last few years.' Point taken: my career as an investigator had meant I wound up standing on some serious toes. Not part of the job description, and most people wondered if I was just plain unlucky or courted the kind of reputation that most criminals would be happy to put on their CV.

'Just tell me.'

'It wasn't Tayside. Although more than a

few of the lads wish they'd been the ones to notice the alleged inconsistencies. Have to wonder what they think of me, eh? They gave it over to a new detective, name of Kellen. Don't know her well. Think she might have transferred after my ... incident. But the request itself, to re-open the investigation, came from an outside agency.'

'Outside? From where?'

'SCDEA.'

SCDEA.

They've gone after the biggest and baddest Scotland has to offer. But it's tough to tell how much difference an organization like that really makes when they take so many years to build a case against the real bastards. The truly untouchable.

Like David Burns.

SCDEA had enough files on Burns to build another headquarters.

But all those files were useless. Only so much paper. Because the law is reliant on evidence and proof. To take down a man like Burns you need proof of his guilt beyond a reasonable doubt. The evidence was circumstantial. At best.

When you tried to take down a man like Burns, you ran the risk of things going wrong. And they always did when the authorities came close to the old bugger. Key witnesses refused to talk or changed their stories at the last minute. Known associates claimed the old man to be utterly innocent. They had acted of their own accord, and he had nothing to do with it. Sometimes investigating officers with their own secrets would develop a change of heart, or those who managed to live the lives they preached would find the shite pouring in from above, from places over which they had no control.

The old man insulated himself well. But always managed to rub his guilt in the faces of those who wanted him behind bars. Letting them know how much he enjoyed their frustration.

To get to him, you needed to turn someone he trusted. A person who had his ear, his respect.

Made sense.

And it made sense that the SCDEA would look into me. Burns and I had a long, complex history, but it was clear that he had a strange fascination with me. More than once he'd asked me to work for him. He'd told me to my face how we were the same, his tone like a father who just found his long-lost son.

I wondered how far up in the agency Griggs had to go to sanction his scheme. How long had it taken him to realize that I was the man for his job? Maybe he'd been looking at me for a long time, just waiting until I was close enough to desperate that he could approach me. Or it's just possible I was his last hope; a final, desperate throw of the dice.

Either way, getting close to Burns was the last thing I wanted to do. I was finally putting my life back together. And even with Susan gone, the idea that she would come back kept me going. Susan had stuck by me through all the bad shite, and while she needed her own space for now, I thought that we might be good for each other.

That maybe the timing was right.

If I went along with Griggs's scheme, it would be a step backwards. I was not the same man I had been when I killed a London thug in the midst of a thunderstorm. I was not the same man I had been when I lied to the police about my involvement with David Burns.

I was someone better. Someone stronger.

And I didn't want to go back.

Griggs was staying at the Apex Hotel, down near the old docks.

It's an odd-looking building, just across from the Quayside shopping complex. The Quayside is one of those developments that never quite took off. It was meant to be a new shopping hub, but the shops were never too popular, and the only business that seemed to thrive was the Chinese Buffet. A few contenders had moved there in recent years including a pizza franchise and an Indian restaurant, but something about the whole place had the sad air of a potential that was never realized.

The Apex Hotel overlooks both the old docks and the shopping complex. Whoever had the bright idea of putting wood panels on the upper levels never really thought through what the strong winds and proximity to the Tay would do. The wood hasn't aged well, and the structure still looks temporary. But inside, it's a small slice of luxury.

I stood outside one of the rooms on the upper floor, and knocked. Hard.

When the door opened, Griggs said, 'How'd you find me?'

'I'm a detective. You didn't make it difficult.'

He nodded. Stood aside to let me in.

The room was a suite, the bed cordoned off from the rest of the room, the main living area all hardwood floors and elegant furniture. He grabbed a long-backed chair. I sat on the sofa. Kept my body language loose, showing him I wasn't afraid.

He smiled.

'You worked it out, then?'

'I don't remember you being this underhanded. They give you courses at the agency?'

'Times change. People change.'

I let that one hang in the air.

'What happens if I don't agree to your proposal?'

He stood up, went to the mini-bar. Grabbed a couple of beers, lifted one in the air and waggled it in my direction. When I didn't respond, he tossed the bottle. I caught it easy, unscrewed the top.

He drank standing next to the bar.

I waited.

He said, 'There's no one left on your side. Any allies you had were lost during that incident last year.'

Incident.

He was talking about when I exposed the deputy chief constable, Kevin Wood, as a drug-dealing arsehole. The force was still reeling. He'd been one bad apple, but everyone felt the repercussions from his actions. More than that, everyone was at a loss to explain how he had risen so far up the ranks.

Some folk wondered if I had doctored the evidence. Those people were looking for any excuse to take me down. That was where I initially assumed the heat came from. Now I knew better, of course.

Looking at Griggs, I wondered whether he'd been the one to tip off Cameron Connelly. The two had history. Griggs had been there when Connelly lost the use of his legs.

'And if I agree?'

'Then it goes away. When you're done.'

'When I'm done?'

40

'We need you on Burns's good side. He needs to believe that you have abandoned your principles. That you're bitter and angry enough to finally accept what he has to offer.'

'I've seen *The Departed*,' I said. 'I know how this ends.'

Griggs laughed.

I didn't.

'You want to take him down the same as me,' Griggs said. 'Maybe more so.'

'I'm not a copper any more. I don't want to join the SCDEA. I just want to live my life.'

'It's a pity you're not an alcoholic,' he said. 'That would help with the cover.'

'Or turn me into a crying, walking, talking living cliché.'

'To misquote Cliff.'

'If I accept your offer,' I said, 'there's going to be impact on my business. My life. Even if you clear me of any wrongdoing, when this is over there will still be people who can't forget the things I would have to do working for that fucker.'

'Think on it,' Griggs said. 'I'm not a complete bastard. There's a handsome retainer. Enough to cover any loss of expenses.'

He was a cold bastard.

Had he always been like this?

Or was it just for my benefit?

Back when I knew him, I'd been a uniform. More, I'd been green. Still learning the

41

ropes. He'd been a legend on the force; the man who'd seen some of the worst shite that the world could throw at a copper. He'd been investigated by Discipline and Complaints at least once regarding his methodology. And yet he came through it all smelling of roses.

The man I remembered was decent. Honourable, even.

Had that all been a cover?

Or worse, had I been too blinded by the legend to see the man?

I swigged back the beer, then stood up. 'Sorry,' I said. 'I'm going to pass.'

'Let the dice fall as they may?'

'You should get out more,' I said. 'Stop reading books and watching TV. Maybe make you better at persuasion.'

He didn't stop me leaving, but I have a feeling now that he already knew what was going to happen. And I wonder if he even felt the tiniest moment of regret or human conscience.

Downstairs, in the lobby, two guys in jeans and white shirts got up from a leather sofa and walked over to me as I exited the lift. I clocked the way they walked – faux-cowboy gait that looked like a bad case of rickets – and knew where they'd come from.

'Mr McNee?'

No point in pissing about: 'He knows I

don't want to talk to him.'

The bigger of the two – he had a baby-like face that might have been jolly if it wasn't pitted with the marks of the teenage-acne veteran – blinked a couple of times. Trying to figure how I knew who they were.

His companion was smaller, thinner, with a lip that constantly curled upwards in a poor attempt at a sneer. Thought he looked badass. Looked more like he had a bad cold sore inside his upper lip. He didn't care whether I knew who they were or how. Just said, 'When he wants to see you, pal, you go and see him. What you want doesn't bloody well enter into it.'

I could have laid them both out. Over the last few years, I'd been in my share of fights, and these two weren't in the best of shape.

But we were in a public place.

And I was realizing that I'd just been play-ed by Griggs. What I wanted from life really didn't matter any more.

I was a pawn.

But I still wasn't sure quite whose side of the board I was on.

FIVE

I followed them out to the east of the city. Not that I needed directions. I knew where we were going. The last place I wanted to be.

Burns's house was ex-council, but he'd expanded it so that the house stuck out from those around it, made you realize that here lived a man who loved his neighbourhood, but had risen above his neighbours.

Police statistics claimed that Burns's street was one of the most crime-free in the city. Officially, this was just a statistical anomaly, or perhaps even proof that the local force were doing their job pretty damn well. The unofficial reason, and the one that made far more sense, was that no one in their right mind wanted to cross the old man or his family. A few years ago, some kids with grand ambition and little sense tried dealing drugs around the corner from the Burns family home. The schmucks had died hurting, their assailants never caught, their stash stuffed into broken, dead jaws.

I parked outside, just behind the car I'd

followed, took a deep breath before getting out. The old man sat in a lawn chair outside his front door, sipping a beer. Waved it at me as I opened his front gate and walked up to him.

'Fair weather,' he said. 'We should enjoy it while it lasts.'

'Scottish summer,' I said. 'Ten minutes of sunshine a year.'

'We'd complain if it was too hot,' he said. 'But you know, this isn't about the weather, son.' He sipped at his beer. Closed his eyes and let loose a long sigh. The way he sat, you'd think he was just another pensioner enjoying his retirement. Here, close to his family, he was just another old man enjoying the later years. You'd never imagine this was the same man who, in his youth, had nailed a priest who owed him money to a cross inside his own church. You'd never imagine that this serene old man had ordered the deaths of people he'd never even met, had spilt blood with his own hands.

I waited for his pitch. It was coming sooner or later. Always did, with Burns. He'd been obsessed with me for years. Claiming he saw something of himself in me. Perhaps because his own son had turned out so different from him. He was looking for a replacement. Decided I would be the best candidate.

First time anyone ever thought that about me. And it had to be the meanest old bastard

I'd ever met.

Burns opened his eyes to look at me. 'What did Griggs want? A recruitment drive?'

'He has it in for you,' I said. 'Something personal?'

'Old business,' said Burns. 'Men like Griggs have long memories. So, are we to see you decamping to the west coast? Off to join the good fight with the men and women of the SCDEA?'

I shook my head.

'You'd be missed,' he said. 'By some folks.' Adding that last bit like an afterthought, making sure I knew he wouldn't get too sentimental.

'What do you want?'

'Friendly warning. That's all,' he said. 'I wouldn't trust Griggs as far as you could punt him. He's not above pulling out dirty tricks if the mood takes him.'

'I worked with him for a few years,' I said. 'He was a good man.'

'Listen to yourself,' said Burns. '*Was*. People change.'

'You're not the first person to tell me that today.'

He sipped at his beer. 'I've always respected you, but sometimes you can be a real pain in the arse, McNee. Anyone else, I'd know their price. What they wanted. What they desired. But you, I don't know you as well as I used to think I did.'

'I'm full of surprises.'

'I'm sure you are.' He smiled. 'But know this: I've let you run around free for the past few years. Even as you called me names and slapped my hand away when I only offered friendship. But if you even think about working with a shitebag like Griggs, then it's over. No more Mr Nice Guy. You and me, we should have been friends, McNee.'

It was the same old pitch, with a whole new angle. The tone was no longer paternal. It was aggressive, adversarial. Griggs had the old man worried. Which told me that the detective was a serious man. That his offer to me had been serious. If he had done enough already to rattle Burns, then he had to have an end game in mind.

And he also had to know that Burns would be watching me.

How much did the old man know about what the fair-haired copper had offered me? Did he know about the undercover operation?

They were stuck in their own cold war, Griggs and Burns, both aware of what the other was up to, but afraid to make a move in case they showed their hand.

'If that's it, then,' I said and turned to leave, thinking about asking him for money for wasted petrol.

But I didn't.

And he didn't have any last moment words

of parting advice.

Burns always liked to have the last word. His silence was more threatening than anything he could have said.

SIX

When I got back to work, a woman was waiting for me. She sat patiently in reception, hands placed lightly on her lap, back straight, eyes staring at something no one else could see. Dot was over at her computer, not working too hard to disguise her discomfort.

'I told Mrs Farnham that you would call her to arrange an appointment, but she insisted on waiting.'

The name sounded familiar. I tried to figure if I knew her face. She was dressed in dark colours, and the way she sat made me think of a woman in mourning. Her lipstick was dark red against pale skin and her hair was close to black, although the lines in her face and the skin on her neck gave her age away. Her earrings were heavy but not ostentatious. She could have stepped out of the 1950s with her fashion sense.

We'd met before. But I couldn't place her.

Memories were bubbling somewhere in my mind. But they weren't breaking the surface.

She stood. Didn't offer a hand. Maybe she expected me to recognize her. But there was no expression on her face for me to read. I sensed a sadness in her, but it wasn't recent. It was old, had become a part of her. 'I just need five minutes of your time.'

I ushered her into my office and shut the door. Offered her a seat and a drink. She took the seat. Same straight-backed pose as outside in reception.

I perched on the edge of the desk. Informal. 'Before we even begin, I should tell you that I am currently on suspension from the Association of British Investigators.'

'Suspension?'

'There have been allegations made against this company. I am legally obliged to—'

'Are they true?'

'No.' The word slipped out. I hadn't known how I'd respond to the question.

She nodded. 'Then I'm fine with that.'

I must have looked confused. She said, 'You have a good face, Mr McNee. A little sad, maybe, but good. It's not scientific, really, but I have found you can tell a lot about a person by their face. Besides, I know you. I remember you. You were a kind man.'

The bubbles in my brain broke the surface. Memories took on recognizable shapes. I remembered her name. 'I'm sorry. I didn't ... it's been a long time. You're Elizabeth Farnham?'

Her head bowed.

I stood up. An automatic reflex. A strange

50

kind of attempt to show respect for the be-
reaved.

It had been almost six years, now.

So much had happened since I last saw
her.

'How can I help you?'

She licked her lips, as though suddenly
dehydrated. She could no longer look me in
the eyes.

She said, 'You can find my son's killer. You
can clear Alex Moorehead's name.'

I wished I'd kept the beer that Griggs had
given me earlier. Or asked for something
stronger.

Justin Farnham had been ten years old when
he disappeared.

He lived with his mother – his father, her
husband, had left six years previously with a
blonde ten years his junior – in a small village a few miles outside the city. The village
was tight-knit, and if it had been the 1950s
and not the 2000s, everyone would have
kept their doors unlocked at all times, wan-
dered freely in and out of each other's
houses with a cheery 'good morning'.

Elizabeth Farnham had been frantic with
worry. She'd told her son to come back at a
certain time, but he never did.

She told the police he'd been out playing
with some friends in the fields. They liked to
play among the farmer's bales, jumping from

51

one to the other, hiding in the nooks and crannies, playing acrobatic games of tig. Once or twice, they hurt themselves. One of the kids had cracked a collar bone after mistiming a jump. But that was just the way things were; kids played and sometimes they hurt themselves. No parent can protect their child for ever.

But Elizabeth always told her son that he had to stay with other kids, that he couldn't go off on his own or with a stranger. He'd always been sensible, but when Mrs Farnham rang some of the other parents, she found their kids had been home on time.

Only Justin was missing.

Three hours later, she called the police. We responded quickly. A missing child is every parent's and copper's worst nightmare. Logistically and emotionally.

The search brought out everyone in the local community. Elizabeth Farnham's direct neighbour – a freelance IT technician called Alex Moorehead – spearheaded much of the local effort. He was a relatively young man, well liked by everyone in the village, although he was regarded as something of an oddball. No one ever knew him to have a girlfriend or any other kind of significant other. It wasn't the kind of village where accusations of homosexuality would result in ostracism, and the generally perceived belief was that Alex simply didn't have an interest in sex with anyone.

The cops took to him like a hunting dog who'd tasted blood.

I say the cops, I mean Ernie Bright.

He got the scent fast.

I remember seeing it in his eyes, first time he met Moorehead.

I was there to observe only; part of Ernie's plan to groom me for CID.

Moorehead fitted the stereotypical profile.

Single.

No reported sexual preference.

Computer geek.

Regarded as pleasant enough but no one knew him.

Occam's razor?

Maybe.

But it was more than just snapshot profiling. Ernie sensed something about Moorehead; an uneasiness that set him apart from the crowd. If he wasn't directly responsible, then he knew *something*.

It was Moorehead who found the body. He was leading a search party out in the woods near the field where the kids had been playing. At the head of the pack, sweeping slowly with a long stick to move aside the grass and plantlife. When he found the body, he was reported to be out of view of the rest of the party, yelling back, 'Over here! I've found ... Oh God, I think it's him! It's Justin!'

That kind of thing, it sets alarm bells ring-ing. When something seems too coincidental or simply too good to be true, it usually is. Most crimes of passion, the perpetrator will go out of their way to get caught, acting in ways that draw attention to them, even if it seems like misdirection.

That was the second strike against Moorehead in Ernie's eyes. Not enough to take him in for questioning, but enough to make him a person of interest, as they say in the trade.

Justin's body was buried under a pile of leaves and grass. Six days out in the open had taken its toll on the corpse, and when the funeral was eventually held, the casket had to be closed.

'He's a cool customer,' Ernie said, meaning Moorehead. He told me this as we watched the crime-scene technicians investigate the area around the body, while the villagers all stood at the edge of the crime-scene tape and watched with disbelief as we investigated the death of one of their own. 'Finding that body the way he did, he should have been ... I don't know, but he shouldn't have been cold like that. It was a performance, McNee. I know it. Feel it in my gut.'

Still, we didn't talk to Moorehead. We couldn't. We'd have brought the wrath of our superiors down on our heads. You don't accuse a man without evidence. Without something more substantial than a simple gut feeling.

Elizabeth Farnham appeared on television several times over the next few weeks, paraded around news outlets and daytime TV like a performing animal. She looked like she barely knew where she was, and she told her story so many times that by the time the police finally arrested Moorehead, she sounded numbed and distant from the re-telling.

When she appeared, she would plead not only for any witnesses to what had happened, but for the killer to admit the truth and turn themselves in. For months, before I fell asleep, I could hear her words echo around my head: *Please do this, not for me or for my boy, but for yourself. I am sure you regret what you did. I am sure you did not mean to kill him. Come forward and admit what you did.*

They say confession is good for the soul.

But no one confessed.

And Ernie continued to focus on Alex Moorehead as a 'person of interest'.

Moorehead had been out of the others' sight when the body was discovered. A fact that added more detail to Ernie's picture of Moorehead as a man with an agenda in finding the body.

Alex cooperated with us. We took him to the station several times, questioned him in his home. He answered every question without hesitation. Cooperated fully.

Said more than once that an innocent man

had nothing to hide.

But something was wrong.

Ernie was right. Alex Moorehead was too calm and collected. Unconcerned.

Every regret expressed for what happened to Elizabeth Farnham was mechanical. He acted like a man coached in innocence. He was too perfect. As Ernie would say at the trial, he had been 'inappropriately distant', given that he was the one to find the body.

Not a crime in itself. Especially for a computer geek.

Ernie continued to drive the investigation towards Moorehead, finally procuring a warrant to search the man's property. Raising enough questions that the DCI in charge couldn't continue to hem and haw regarding the strength of Ernie's gut. We didn't find the murder weapon – a 'blunt, round-edged instrument' according to forensic reports – and of course we didn't find any DNA on the young boy's body. The lack of evidence pointed towards someone who had planned this particular attack for a long time.

Which was why Moorehead's PC broke the case.

We found several pictures of kids from the village. Nothing too disturbing, but the majority were long-angle shots clearly taken without the participant's knowledge.

The photographs gave us cause to check the drive for hidden and deleted data. No matter how hard you try and wipe a computer, there's always something recoverable on there. A second, deeper sweep through Moorehead's hard drive revealed more pictures of children, these downloaded from the darker recesses of the internet. This second sweep was performed by an outside contractor, who would later admit to an old friendship with the accused, but who had come recommended by the DCI in charge of the case, Kevin Wood. All of this would happen around the time I was forced off the case and eventually off the job by an accident that would echo through the rest of my life. Run off the road by a driver who was never caught.

The second set of images they found on Moorehead's PC was in a very different category to the first set. Graphic. Explicit. Appealing to a debased kind of sexuality that most people could never hope to understand.

Moorehead pleaded innocent to possession of indecent images. But he couldn't provide an explanation as to where the images found in his machine had come from. Not that it mattered. They were there. They hadn't been downloaded in innocence. Too many images. Too frequent dates for that. No one else had access to his machine.

Ernie and Wood brought the hammer down.

Moorehead was indicted on two separate charges. The first being possession of indecent images. The second being the murder of Justin Farnham. The case was passed up to the High Court of Justiciary, where it seemed for a while that Moorehead might dispute the charges brought against him.

On the charge of possessing the images found on his computer, he claimed to be not guilty. But then, as the proceedings rumbled forward and the fifteen-person jury was brought before the Lord Commissioner of Justiciary, Moorehead broke his silence on the death of Justin Farnham.

Guilty.

He broke down in court. Pled to the higher charge of murder. There was no choice left but to sentence him to life. Twenty-five years. The commissioner gave him fifteen years punishment on the life sentence. Meaning that once those fifteen years were up, he could apply for bail on licence.

No one thought he would apply. Moorehead seemed determined to serve out his sentence. Life for a life.

Inside, he spent much of his time in solitary confinement. For his own safety.

Most prisoners detest anyone convicted for harm to a child. The worst and most violent sociopaths will cry and rail for the return of the death penalty for these prisoners, some even claiming that they give criminals a bad name. I understand that. Certain crimes are worse than others. Even the most hardened thug has a basic code of morality and conduct. Even they would think twice before harming a child.

There were always going to be unanswered questions, of course. Such as why Moorehead pleaded innocent to the charge of possessing indecent images, and yet failed to provide a reasonable – or even unreasonable – excuse for the pictures found on his PC.

But none of that mattered. They had their man. Ernie and I had talked to him on multiple occasions before I left the case. As I watched the trial unfold in the media, I was more than satisfied as to his guilt.

Soon after Moorehead was sentenced, something strange happened. Other forces came forward with cases, child abduction, even murder. All of them unsolved. All of them taking place near where Moorehead had been staying at the time. Moorehead was only thirty-eight but the cases went back around fifteen years, just after his graduation.

Project Amityville became a full-time job. Ernie couldn't take it, handed the gig over to Fife Police willingly, as they had at least three cases where Moorehead was now the most likely suspect.

Moorehead offered little or no help with these new investigations. The officers assigned to Amityville had to try and work with next to nothing to prove that he was in some way responsible for a string of murders and possible murders dating back years.

Project Amityville was still running, nearly six years after Moorehead's arrest. Same cop in charge. He had tangentially tied Moorehead to at least three other cases, suspected his involvement in at least six more. But, like Ernie before him, he found the work like butting his skull against a brick wall. The more he suspected, the more the evidence became circumstantial. Without Moorehead's assistance or admission of guilt, there was often little that could be done.

Occasionally, true-crime newspaper specials or TV docs would resurrect images of Moorehead for after-the-fact speculation. They had called me once or twice for comment, but I refused to talk about the case. All I wanted to do was forget it. In my mind, I equated the Moorehead investigation with the accident that led to my leaving the force. Hardly what you'd call a high note.

Sometimes, late at night on TV, they would show footage of Elizabeth Farnham as she had been – the grieving, distraught mother, unable to properly display her grief after being put in the full glare of not only the police but also the media investigation into her son's death.

★ ★ ★

That was how I remembered her. The late-night TV docs that still obsessed over the unanswered questions of the Moorehead investigation froze my image of her as she had been six years ago.

I recall her saying, with the sharp hatred that only comes from the greatest of losses, that we needed to return to the death penalty, just this once, and show men like Moorehead that there were consequences for their actions.

And now she was telling me that she believed he was innocent?

Why the change of heart?

'All due respect,' I said, 'but he's guilty. They proved that he was—'

She held up a hand. 'I didn't believe it when they told me. In that shocked way that later turned to hatred. I thought, it can't be Alex. No, it can't be. He was a good neigh-bour. An oddball, yes, but a psycho? A mur-derer? A killer of children? But then I started to question my doubts. And I believed everything I saw in the newspapers or heard from your people. I hated Alex Moorehead. Despised him. But over the years, I thought more and more about what happened. Not what happened to Justin, but in the course of your investigation. As kind and determined as you were to find the killer, I have to wonder if maybe you weren't a little too determined. The minute your boss questioned Alex, he was marked for the crime. And then ... those pictures the media showed of him. One look at those and you'd think he really was a psychopath.'

I remembered the images. The minute his name had leaked as a person of interest – I always suspected it had been done on purpose, to try and draw him out – the papers had photographers hanging outside his house, trying to catch the most guilty looking snap they could. And they really nailed him. Early morning, taking out the bins, no one looks at their best, and in Alex Moorehead's case, it was the eyes that did it. He was a young man, but his eyes were surrounded by heavy bags and wrinkles. No doubt the result of sitting up late in the evening, staring at code or the flashing images of the latest console game. Or, if you believed the charges, images of children that would turn the stomach of anyone with an ounce of common morality.

'We connected him to other cases, and—'

She nodded, and I realized she'd heard all this before, maybe even made the counter-arguments herself. I'd barged into the conversation, forgetting one of the primary rules of the investigation gig – let the client do the talking.

So I stopped talking, sat back. Let her continue.

'I went to see him,' she said. 'After all these

years, I went to see him. I wanted to look him in the eye and ask what had happened to all those other children, and please, couldn't he let their mothers know what had happened to them. Because as horrific as the truth was bound to be, it couldn't be worse than the not knowing.' She lifted her head, again, and took a deep breath. Her hands, still on her lap, remained perfectly still. 'I asked him, and I looked him in the eyes. Like I said, Mr McNee, I like to think I'm a good judge of character, that I can read people's faces. And what his face told me was that he was innocent. That for all these years, he has been saying nothing, because I believe he genuinely knows nothing.'

SEVEN

Much as I tried to talk her out of it, Elizabeth Farnham insisted I at least talked to Moorehead. If I thought she was crazy, she'd leave it alone. I even raised my fees a little to try and put her off, but she wasn't backing down.

'I remembered you. You hung on the senior detective's word, but I think you had your doubts.'

Of course I had my doubts. But I was younger then. Less sure of myself. And Ernie was a copper's copper, the kind of man I wanted to be. I had to trust his instincts over mine.

Could he have been wrong?

Something about Mrs Farnham's insistence made those old doubts resurface. And given what I had discovered about Ernie the year before, I had to wonder if he hadn't made a few mistakes since then.

As human as the rest of us.

Which was how I found myself pulling on a dark suit and tie the next morning. Driving to the Category A unit at Perth Prison.

64

I had some pull with one of the senior wardens. An ex-cop, he was one of the few who still talked to me. Perhaps because his new career had kept him insulated from some of my more recent missteps. When I rang his house, he asked why I only ever called when I needed a favour. I told him it was because I was a parasite and he didn't laugh.

But he didn't berate me, either.

There was a plastic wall between myself and Moorehead. Given how many people wanted to hurt him – even, now, so many years after he'd been banged up – it was safer for both of us to talk that way. When he spoke into the microphone, his voice was soft, barely above a whisper. 'I remember you.'

'My name's McNee.'

'The junior detective, right? Finally got your badge?'

'I'm not police any more. I work private.'

'You here on your own? Or one of them ... hired you?'

'One of who?'

'The mothers.'

'The mothers?'

'Of the disappeared.' Talking about the mothers of his alleged victims. Just being in the same room as him, I got this little shiver running up my spine. He looked like a guilty man, now. His skin was pale. He sat with his head forward and looked up at me as though he couldn't stand to face me head on.

Had he always been like this?

Or had prison changed him?

I tried to remember. To cut out the interpretation of the years, to remember with clarity the man that Alexander Moorehead had once been.

And I failed.

All I remembered was the media monster.

I said, 'I'm here on behalf of someone who thinks you're innocent.'

He gave a little cough. Might have been his version of a laugh. Hard to tell. All the time inside, he'd forgotten how to smile.

'You used to say you were. Innocent, I mean. Always protesting your arrest. And yet never saying a word about how all the evidence managed to damn you so completely. Even now, you've never really talked about any of the other victims. Except Justin.'

He remained silent.

'Someone is willing to believe you. If you are innocent, I'll find the proof.'

'You put me in here. You and your boss.'

'You helped us.'

He sat back in his chair, regarded me with dark, shadowed eyes.

'You act like you want to be here. You want to be locked up.'

'It's better this way,' he said, finally giving me something.

'You're sorry for what happened to Justin?'

66

'Yes.'

'And the other boys?'

Silence

'You're sorry for any mother who has lost their child?'

'Yes.'

'Then give them peace by telling me where the bodies are.'

Back to the mime impersonation. Trying to look bored. But I could sense something else, too. An edgier emotion; something crying out to be released, just beneath that placid surface.

'Or tell me why you don't know. Tell me why you're innocent. Just ... give me something.'

Was I reading too much into his new act? Buying too readily into Elizabeth Farnham's story?

All those years ago, I'd been convinced as to his guilt. But what convinced me was another man's absolute conviction.

Was I doing the same, in reverse, with Elizabeth Farnham, allowing her own absolute certainty to affect my judgement?

'Are we done, now?'

Moorehead had spent ten years stonewalling Project Amityville. Giving them nothing, not even a hint, as to the truth behind those crimes they suspected him of. What would I expect to discover in one morning? One interview?

All I'd wanted was to look at him, see if there was even a hint of what Elizabeth Farnham said she had seen.

Just a hint.

A possibility.

I wanted to see it, too. Perhaps because hopeless causes had become my personal quest in the last few years. And just once, I'd like a chance to turn someone's bad fortune around, to redress the balance of injustice in the world.

The detective in charge of Amityville after Ernie stepped aside was a big guy named Wemyss. He wore plaid shirts, sported a moustache, and had a weakness for mid-morning bacon rolls. Something I took full advantage of when I arranged our meeting in Kirkcaldy, near police HQ.

We ate at a diner a few streets away from the building, drank strong black coffee. Around us, people who would never imagine the kind of things cops could see during the course of an investigation bitched to each other and their mobiles about bosses and spouses.

'There was another investigator I used to know from Dundee,' Wemyss told me after taking the first, big bite out of his roll. His teeth were stained with ketchup. 'Bryson, I think his name was.'

'I took his old business,' I said. 'He was

looking to get out of the country. Move abroad with his partner.'

'Yeah,' said Wemyss. 'Remember hearing something about that. He got in over his head. Guess that can happen, you don't have the support of the force behind you.'

I shrugged. I only knew the guy in passing. Time to get to the reason I was here. 'I still try not to think about what I saw. At Moorehead's place.'

He chewed a few times, swallowed, then took a slow sip of his coffee before answering. The whole time he eyeballed me, trying to figure what kind of man I was. Finally he said, 'Sure. That kind of stuff gives you nightmares. It passes, though. Want to know what's worse? Trying to find out what he actually did. Linking all these murders and disappearances to a man who refuses to talk. The bastard won't confirm or deny anything. He just sits there and looks at me, you know? Every time I go in there to present him with evidence, he just gives me this look like he doesn't hear what I'm saying, see what I'm showing him.'

'I went to see him yesterday.'

'And?'

'And he remembered me. That's about all he said.'

'Little cunt,' Wemyss said, matter of fact. He ripped into his roll with the relish of a starving man. 'Nothing like a good bacon buttie.'

Bacon rolls are the cure for all evils. At least in Scotland. I remember talking to a forensic specialist who confided in me that working murder scenes always gave her a craving for 'the fattiest, greasiest, most butter-soaked buttie you could find'. She couldn't explain it. But it seemed to work for her, helped her to deal with what she did.

Wemyss said, 'Which of them're you working for?'

I played dumb.

He persisted: 'Which of the mothers?'

'Elizabeth Farnham.'

His face screwed up, like he thought he'd maybe misheard.

I said, 'She thinks Moorehead is innocent.'

He took a moment to digest his food, and what I'd told him. 'Fucksakes,' he said. 'I didn't think she'd actually carry this through.'

Elizabeth Farnham didn't come running to me the second she thought that Moorehead was innocent of killing her boy or any of the others. She went to Wemyss first. Told him what she'd told me: that she looked into Moorehead's eyes and understood that he really didn't know anything.

'Gut instinct isn't a natural thing,' Wemyss told me as we walked through the front doors of Kirkcaldy FHQ. 'Takes years of practice. Know what I mean?' I resisted the urge to make a joke about guts, figured a man of his size had heard them all before. Besides, I was playing nice. Not a game I was used to, of course.

I said, 'What do you think about Moorehead?'

'That he's guilty. He's hiding something.'

I tried for flippant: 'Everybody's hiding something.'

The big man didn't look at me, but if I wasn't careful I'd have been knocked down by the sheer strength of his disgust.

Project Amityville was stationed in a room on the third floor, tucked away to the rear of the building. Anonymous. The walls a neutral beige. The furniture temporary. Had been temporary for over five years now. But that's what happens with these cases. You can begin with all the enthusiasm you like, but sooner or later they become a never-ending slog; the copper equivalent of a Sisyphean punishment. How many times had Wemyss pushed the rock up that hill?

What struck me about the incident room were the images and charts that did their best to hide that anonymity, forcing your attention on them as you entered the room.

At least ten different faces I could see pinned to the boards. All young boys, all smiling, all happy. All around ten years old. Between them, hand-written suppositions,

71

copies of evidence, circled transcripts, and pictures of their mothers. Some of those photographs looking like before and after shots for what grief can do to you given enough time and heft.

I tried to speak, but couldn't say anything. Humbled by what this place represented.

Wemyss said, 'All of these boys, I know that Moorehead killed them. Show him any one of these pictures and you can see a reaction. Even if he tries to hide it. He flinches, looks away.'

'Doesn't want to admit what he's done.'

Wemyss nodded. His eyes moved from one dead boy to the next. I got the feeling that this had become a habit, a ritual for him every time he entered this room. A way of reminding himself what he was doing and why. His expression didn't change. Maybe he was immune to feelings of despair. Numbed to the horror of what it meant for a life to be snuffed out before it even had a chance.

'It's not a new story,' he said. 'Man does something he can't face up to, denies it until the denial becomes his truth. But just beneath the surface, the guilt remains. He can't get rid of it. Can't wipe it away like a file on a computer.' He turned to face me. 'Alex Moorehead killed those boys. And one day he'll admit it. He won't have any choice.'

He was absolutely certain. Utterly convincing.

Like Ernie all those years ago. He was desperate to find closure for the women whose children were frozen for ever on the wall of this incident room. And I had to wonder if that meant he couldn't allow himself the luxury of doubt.

'I'm sorry I wasted your time,' I told him.

'You're not the first, McNee,' he said. 'And you won't be the last.'

EIGHT

I had two missed calls on my mobile, from the same number. One message waiting.

Sandy Griggs.

I figured this was what it was to have a stalker.

I could have deleted the message, but instead let it play, listened to it while looking out the side window of the car, into the shadow of old industrial buildings that had fallen into disuse.

'McNee, give some thought to my offer. I know it's asking a lot, and maybe you think I'm trying to paint you into a corner, but I need you to understand how important your cooperation is to...'

I let him ramble on.

Didn't call back.

He could wait. Sweat it out.

Meantime, I had a real job to attend to. A real client.

Wemyss had tried to dissuade me from looking deeper into Alex Moorehead. Maybe he genuinely believed there was nothing more to be found. Maybe he was fed up of

74

people like me stepping on his toes.

Either way, I wasn't going backing down.

It was a fault in my thinking; a defect, maybe. I just couldn't let something go until I had examined it from every angle. More importantly, I couldn't leave a job knowing I'd given it a half-arsed attempt.

Susan called it a chronic desire to please people. I called it keeping promises.

And with Elizabeth Farnham, it was something more. If there was even a chance that me and Ernie had made a mistake when we arrested Alex Moorehead for killing her son, then it had to be examined. I needed to clear this up.

For her peace of mind.

And mine.

Early afternoon, back in Dundee, I locked myself in the office with the coffee machine perking and the remnants of a sandwich from a shop near the university campus.

What I did was fire up the machine, hit Google and enter 'Alex Moorehead' into the search box.

Once I got rid of the estate agent and would-be author/singer/actor websites, the major hits came from true-crime sites. There were a few videos on YouTube of old documentaries. I watched them intently, fast-forwarding the talking heads and focusing on footage from home videos and news reports from outside the court.

I watched old footage of me and Ernie, mostly as we tried to avoid the cameras and just do our job.

Later, I was replaced in the footage by Kevin Wood. Getting front and centre for the cameras. Overshadowing Ernie.

Ernie hated talking to the media. He'd been burned more than once early in his career, quickly decided that the press loved nothing more than finding ways to fuck up an investigation. Didn't matter about justice, long as they got a good story. Wood, on the other hand, understood the power of the press. He gave interviews when asked, always had a sound bite. He came across as a political animal, someone who understood the power in forming good relations with the right people.

Watching the footage was like walking into a house you hadn't been in for years, and turning the lights on one by one. Slowly, I started to remember small details, reconnecting bits and pieces of information that had become disparate with the passing of years.

Memory is an imperfect thing. Ideas and sensations that seem crystal clear degrade and change with time. They merge with other memories, become something that bears no resemblance to the truth.

I had simplified the Moorehead case in my

head, forgotten all the quirks, peculiarities and unanswered questions.

The biggest problem we had was that Moorehead had very few strikes against his name. His dark side had been utterly hidden. You could make the argument that it was so hidden, it might never have been there at all.

According to several of the documentaries, he stayed off the radar because he was rarely in one force's jurisdiction for long enough for any alarm bells to ring. The nature of his work – a freelance IT specialist – meant that he was always looking for the next job and that he rarely made any ties where he stayed. He would get in, work the contract, get out. His life was lived in a variety of rented homes.

He had no real roots. Went out of his way to ensure he didn't accidentally create any.

But then, a lot of people live like that. And I had to wonder if the commentators weren't stretching, trying to look for motive or planning where there was none.

I looked at pictures over and over again. The famous ones. The obscure ones. The family snapshots. His parents had been quick to disown their son, his mother refusing to talk to the press at all, his father speaking only in short, declarative sentences about how disappointed he was in his boy.

The mother had died three years ago.

Heart attack. Sudden. Unexpected. Brought Moorehead briefly back into the news again.

The tabloids made a great deal of the fact that he did not attend her funeral.

His father was, by all accounts, still alive.

Didn't take much to find the man. He was living in a small village just across the border. Phone number and street address were easy enough to find.

Contrary to popular opinion, most eyes do investigative work sitting on their arses. The modern world has allowed us to become sedentary creatures. To quote the old adverts, we let our fingers do the walking.

Way more than we do our legs.

Which is why a gym membership can be essential to the job. If only I could convince the accountant it was tax deductible.

After tracking down Jonathan Moorehead, I decided I'd give him a call. There were a lot of unanswered questions regarding their relationship, and I found it interesting that he had refused to even talk to his son after the lad's arrest.

He answered in six rings. His voice was deep, cracking with age, but still gruff and severe. I remembered sitting in a room with him, explaining why we thought he might have more luck than us at getting his son to open up.

'He can go hang,' was all that Jonathan Moorehead had to say. He'd been a big man, big hands. In his younger days, I could imagine his son might have found his presence imposing. The little I knew of the family told me they were Protestant, and certainly old Dad had that severe edge to him.

When I explained who I was, he went quiet. Let me finish my spiel and then slowly, for the hard of thinking, told me: 'Never call me again.'

I listened to the dial tone for a while, considered whether the direct approach might be more effective.

My father drove long distances. He was a sales rep for an electronics company, worked the North and Scotland districts. When I was young, he'd take me with him in the car. I'd sit in the back seat and read books or play games.

The kind of thing you probably couldn't get away with now. But I never minded. I'd lose myself in the books, create my own worlds with games. And chow down at the cafes we'd stop off at along the way.

He told me when I got older that what he liked about the job was that the long distances gave him a chance to think. He'd spend hours in the car thinking about stuff, coming up with solutions to problems.

After his death, I discovered what he'd been thinking about. There were boxes in his house filled with plans and notes on his dream business. He'd spent all the hours in the car thinking about how to proceed, but had never taken that crucial step.

Something about that always made me feel oddly hollow, knowing he had missed out on taking the chance he spent his life chasing. I have often wondered why, what it was that had scared him.

There was so much he had taught me, and that final lesson had been the most important; you need to act, or you'll never achieve anything no matter how much you plan.

I spent the drive south thinking about Alex Moorehead.

It was possible that the man was delusional. Given the nature of his crimes, he was clearly no Joe Citizen. Even if he was mentally competent in the eyes of the law, some switch in his mind was broken.

When did it break? How did it break? Or was there always something wrong with him?

Like a person with an aneurism, some people have deviancies lying dormant, waiting for that one moment when they can finally let loose upon the world.

There is no way to predict when this will happen, or how it will manifest itself.

The idea was terrifying enough in the abstract, but in the case of Alex Moorehead, there had been no real warning signs. Psychologists' reports indicated none of the usual signs of deviancy or violent tendencies.

His actions had been a shock to everyone.

Human beings are the ultimate enigma. All we know of people are what we can see and what they choose to tell us. We do not know – not really – what goes on inside their heads, or how they really see the world. All we can judge on are outward appearances.

For a long time, people believed that you could judge criminals by their appearance. Read early reports by J Edgar Hoover, the man who made America's FBI the force that it is today, and you will see his descriptions of Communist and alien agitators alongside actual career criminals as being identified by their looks, their 'shifty' eyes and general demeanour.

The truth is, most criminals and psychopaths are not identifiable. They could be anyone. Your best friend could be hiding a terrible darkness and you'd never be able to tell.

In the aftermath of terrible events – killing sprees, abuse, massacres – you almost always hear the same thing from neighbours and friends when they talk about the perpetrators. They were quiet, polite, kind, simply not predisposed to this kind of behaviour.

But the public at large and even the media can't understand this. I remembered when Joanna Yeates was murdered in Bristol, the first person the media focused on was her landlord. There was no concrete evidence as to his guilt. They turned on him not simply because the police were talking to him as a person of interest, but because they decided he *looked* like he was guilty. They didn't find the real killer until much later, because the man who killed Joanna did not fit the popular profile of what a murderer should be. The real killer was quiet, ordinary looking and had actually come forward to offer help to the police in their inquiries.

Guilt and innocence are never clear cut or easily defined. Humanity always finds a way to shock and surprise itself. Often in the worst possible ways.

I stopped after about four hours' straight driving at a service station, filled up on cheap, greasy food, watched the people around me.

The best way to understand loneliness is to spend time at a motorway service station. People pass through all the time with no connection or sense of shared humanity. They remain huddled apart, rarely make eye contact. The buzz of arcade machines and the sounds from the overheated kitchens of the always-open hot food stations buzz and ring in your head, remind you not to stay too long. You watch other people and try to make sense of their journey, of why they've needed this temporary stop on the road. And you realize, in the end, that you know nothing about your fellow travellers. That you never will.

My steak pie was flat and unappetizing, the gravy stodgy, barely reheated in the microwave. The chips were half-cooked, the potato inside still crunchy and raw. I chewed at them half-heartedly, wound up leaving half the food behind, feeling disappointed, ripped off and still hungry.

I arrived in the village of Upper Coleman sometime after three. The white-walled houses and quaint upkeep of the gardens made me feel like I'd entered a time capsule. I drove slowly for fear of knocking some flat-capped farmhand off his rusty old bike. The houses all looked the same; everyone afraid to let any sign of age or wear show in case they let the village down.

Rivers End Cottage backed against the stream that ran along the western edge of the village. It was much the same as the others. I only imagined the slight darkness that hung around the windows.

I knocked on the door and waited.

The man who answered was in his early eighties, but he was in good shape and his shoulders were still as broad as I remembered. His skin was turning to leather, but it looked healthy. His eyes were a sharp shade of blue. They looked at me, suspiciously, trying to work out why he knew me.

Jonathan Moorehead had his son just after

he turned forty. Before then, he had shown little interest in being a parent. Many newspapers stated straight out that Alex had been an accident, although none of them even considered calling it a happy one. In some way they thought that very nature of his being unplanned was significant to the way he turned out, as though being a surprise to your parents was the same as being born plain bad. An unexpected baby is a bad one? Maybe I was reading too much between the newsprint. Alex's father was quoted once as saying that perhaps it had been his fault, having a son he never really wanted, but later retracted that statement claiming the reporter in question had 'led me to an answer'.

When he looked at me, standing there on his doorstep, I realized that it wasn't just phone calls he loathed. Unannounced visits were just as high up on his list of hated things.

'Mr Moorehead, we spoke on the phone.' I gave him my name and stated again that I was a private investigator. He moved to close the door on me. 'I'm here because I want to try and prove your son's innocence.'

That got him. Made him hesitate.

It's what they call a foot in the door moment. A moment that I'm always glad is a metaphor.

Finally he relented. Let me inside.

NINE

There were no offers of tea. Not even an invite to sit. Jonathan Moorehead preferred I remain standing. Told me what he thought of my turning up on his doorstep.

His front room was neat and orderly. Knick-knacks lined the bookshelves and the original-feature fire-surround, but they were chosen for the sole purpose of filling the room and making it seem like someone lived here. There was nothing unique. Nothing that spoke of personality. Everything came from brand-furniture warehouses, assembled with Allen keys and fold-out instructions.

The books on the shelves were sparse. Dog-cared Sudoku selections, a large, untouched Collins' dictionary and a couple of thick paperback thrillers that had made the headlines or been turned into big-name movies.

Not a reader, then.

And by the size of the TV, he didn't care too much for his soaps, either.

Begging the question: what did Jonathan

Moorehead do with his days?

The settee where he parked himself while I remained standing was faded, probably a hand-me-down from the house's previous owners or picked up at an auction. The fabric was dark, with a Paisley-style pattern.

The room was hot. Did he ever open the windows?

I thought about how the interior of the house was at such odds with village-idyll exterior.

Had Jonathan Moorehead been like this before his son's arrest? Or was this something that he had been driven to?

Grief changes a person. Sometimes the change is marginal. Even temporary. But it happens. You can't escape it.

The change isn't just exterior, but that's the one most people see. I wonder if it's easier to get over the death of someone you loved than come to terms with the repugnant actions of someone who betrayed you completely.

'How did you find me?'

The question was simple. Direct. Curious. Maybe a little angry.

He had changed his name to Abbott. Clearly thought that was enough. But the paper trail – even in our increasingly paper-less society – had been easy to follow. Unless you're in a government-sponsored programme, or have contacts with special knowledge and the kind of money to get their attention, it's tough to hide away completely. Particularly when someone is determined to track you down.

'I'm an investigator,' I said. 'It's what I do.'

'You were a cop, before. What, you change your mind about my boy when you ... retired?'

I hesitated.

He didn't wait for an answer: 'It's over ten years, Mr McNee. If he was innocent, someone would have found the evidence by now. Would have already known that your boss sent my lad to jail for no reason. But it's not happened. It's not going to happen.' He spoke slowly, kept any anger he felt in check. I could sense it, though, bubbling just beneath the surface. He was old, but his broad shoulders told me he wouldn't be averse to lashing out if the mood took him.

'Are you working for yourself? Is this a personal crusade, protecting psychopaths and perverts you helped put away?'

'No,' I said. 'One of the victims' families hired me. They went to see your son. Seeking closure. They ... thought that by talking to your son they might understand why their boy had to die.'

'And he told them that he was innocent?'

'No.'

'Then what?'

'That's what I'm trying to find out.'

He was silent for a moment. 'My son,' he said, 'killed that boy. Killed all of them, I expect. I've spent the past ten or so years coming to terms with what he did. Don't pretend to understand why. Stopped asking. No answer that could make sense. You know?'

'I know that it hurts you—'

'You don't know anything, Mr McNee. You can't understand that kind of betrayal.'

'No,' I said. 'I can't.'

'He'd be better off dead,' Mr Moorehead said, quiet again, body language loosening, almost in surrender. 'Like a fucking rabid dog.' The words didn't trip naturally from his tongue. He was not a man who swore lightly.

'Bring back hanging?'

'Why not? Too good for the likes of that one.'

A chill descended on the house. A father advocating the death of his own son. Blood is thicker than water?

Aye. Right.

We're bound to family only by expectation. Our bonds are strong only because we work hard to make them so. To admit any kind of negative feeling to our flesh and blood can seem like admitting our weakness.

Which was why it felt odd to hear Mr Moorehead talk about his son like that. His words seemed defensive, maybe even defiant. An act. A show for my benefit.

The house was too warm. My head began to overheat. My brain pushed against my skull. A gentle buzzing started bouncing around inside there like a pissed-off fly.

I said, 'I'm not looking to find out what he was like as a boy. My client doesn't care if she's right or wrong, but feeling uncertain about this is ... it's not a good feeling, Mr Moorehead.'

'I don't know what I can give you. That I didn't already give your boss all those years ago.'

'Do you have anything of Alex's from when he was a boy?'

'I burned everything I had.' He was blinking too much. 'Wouldn't you?'

I looked around. The pictures that sat between the knick-knacks had been bothering me for reasons I couldn't quite determine. Only then did I realize what was wrong: there were no pictures of people. Most folk who live on their own keep pictures of family and friends in some tokenistic fashion. Especially as they get older. Perhaps to remind themselves that they are not alone. But the images on Jonathan Moorehead's shelves were as impersonal as everything else. Postcard images from around the UK, but no faces. No people present at all.

I wondered if he ever talked to anyone any more, aside from the few devoted journalists

89

and true-crime fanatics who inevitably rocked up to his door asking questions just as insensitively as I had.

He hadn't lost a son like Alex Moorehead's victims had. But in a way his grief was every bit as cutting. Every bit as real.

As long as his son was alive, demonized, locked up and still breathing, Jonathan Moorehead couldn't let go or externalize his grief. He couldn't create another fiction for himself. Because his son still existed as a reminder of the truth. Jonathan Moorehead couldn't escape the idea that what had happened was in some way his fault.

I understood when he said his son deserved to be put down.

'Rabid dog' sounded like a right-wing press sound bite. But coming from the man's own father, it sounded like a plea for mercy, as though death was the most tender option when dealing with men who committed crimes such as those Alex Moorehead had been convicted of.

TEN

I wanted to order a pint, but thought I would
need a clear head for the road home. Some
folks drink and drive easily, and when it's a
short trip, I'm not averse to the odd half. But
with the drive in front of me, all I ordered
was a Coke. With my stomach still growling
after the poor quality of the roadside pie, I
ordered the local steak and ale, which the
menu claimed was the Coleman Arms'
speciality.

I ate at the bar. It was only just past four,
and the Arms was hardly a hive of activity.
The middle-aged man with the deliberately
old-fashioned sideburns behind the bar
busied himself shining up the pint glasses.
An old duffer in one corner coughed every
time he turned the page of his newspaper.

'Just visiting?' the barman asked.

'Passing through.'

'Scotchman, eh? What's your line?'

I hesitated. 'Private investigation.'

He nodded, but gave no discernible reaction.

I leaned forward. 'You know if Jonathan

Abbott is a regular round here?'

The bartender shook his head. 'Are you any good at your job? Or is this just a bad day for you?'

'I'm not the first to pass through?'

'It's an open secret. Man wants to live a quiet life. We'd like to let him.'

'I don't want to cause trouble.'

'Then you'll eat your steak and ale and piss off.' He spoke lightly, with a smile at the end of the sentence. But the sentiment was clear. Even if it didn't stop him from taking my custom.

The pie was good. Nothing beats the work of a decent, or at least enthusiastic, chef. I ate in silence, pretended to read one of the papers they had lying on the bar.

The *Sun*.

The Times.

What I was actually doing was playing chicken with the landlord.

Most people in this world want to talk. Even when they tell you to piss off. The thing is, they have this dance they like to do.

People have an innate sense of drama. The same sense that makes gossip so enticing. Details don't really matter, but gossip-masters know all about the power of drama.

The tease. It's all about the tease. Like a good stripper, gossip-masters know that the build-up is as important as the reveal. Expectation is everything.

The bartender was going to talk. He just needed the right incentive. The proper sense of drama.

He finally snapped as I mopped up the gravy with the last of his rustic-cut chips, leaning over the bar with a nervous expression and asking, 'Why're you interested, anyway? Thought there was nothing more to say on the matter. His boy's never going to talk to anyone, right? Taking those poor little buggers to the grave with him, so I hear.'

I chewed slowly. Swallowed. Took a swig of my Coke and then looked up at him. I smiled softly, conspiratorially. 'Thought you didn't want my type round here asking questions?'

'You seem different, mate.'

'Yeah?' I looked around. Conspiratorial. In his mind, I was Bob Woodward, and he was Deep Throat.

The bar was still quiet. The old duffer in the corner was lost in his own world, still reading that newspaper, intent on each and every word in each and every article.

The barman was free to talk.

'Yeah.' He stood back again. 'Call it a gut instinct.'

'I'm working under client confidentiality. I can't possibly comment.'

'You can trust me...'

I hesitated. 'They think he's close to talking,' I said. 'The son.'

'Really?'

'There are conditions, of course. Things that he wants. That he's asked for.'

The bartender's cheeks flushed under those sideburns. He was hitting middle age, would soon start to resemble Mr Bumble from *Oliver Twist* if he wasn't careful. He licked his lips. 'Things?'

'I can't talk about it. But that's why I'm here. Need to talk to the father. Unofficially, of course. You know how it is.'

He nodded. I don't think he really did know what I meant, but he was desperate to be part of something grander and more exciting than the everyday grind.

'Thing is,' I said. 'His old man won't talk to me. And who can blame him? I'm just trying to find a way to get him to open up.'

'Don't think there's much chance of that,' said the bartender. 'I mean everyone knows who he is, but it's an open secret. We just call him Mr Abbott when we see him. No one's got the balls to actually say what they know.'

'You all just recognized him?'

'In a place like this, word travels fast. Heard it on the grapevine, know what I mean?' He leaned forward again. All I had to do now was look interested, guide him occasionally, and I'd get what I needed. Which was context. Background. A sense that my visit here wasn't entirely wasted. 'It was the Mrs noticed first. She loves the true-crime stuff. Has this whole bookshelf of books about unsolved cases, famous killers, all the rest of it. Not sick stuff, mind. But she reckons she should have been a cop rather than a chef.'

'I think she's better off being a chef. Copper's life isn't what it is on telly.'

'That's what she says,' he replied, and laughed. We were still mates, here. My newfound friend was looking relaxed, convinced I wasn't some sicko in town to make trouble. 'But, yeah, she recognized him. And then pretty much everyone did. But he can't help it, you know? His son's a psycho. Got to be tough. He just wants to be left alone, know what I mean?'

'Yeah, I understand.'

'No one's ever really brought it up, face to face, I mean. Why would you? Long as he keeps his house in step with everyone else, everyone around here figures he can keep as much to himself as he likes.'

'That's the important thing round here? Keeping your house in good nick?'

'We've won Best Kept Village three years out of six.'

'I see.'

'Matter of pride.'

'So's your steak and ale pie.'

'I'll tell Mo that,' he said. 'But yeah, he doesn't really get out much into village life. Aside from occasionally popping into a coffee morning.'

'He drink in here?'

'He came in once or twice when he first arrived. Think he was trying to fit in, like, but maybe he knew that we knew who he was. Pleasant enough, though. Liked the steak and ale, too.'

'Man of taste. Maybe I'll open with that. Give us some common ground.'

'That's what I'd do, but I'm no detective.'

'He doesn't socialize with anyone, then?'

'No, not really. Well, Mrs Hutton. She runs the newsagent's, like. He has a standing order there for his papers and magazines. Does crosswords and the like.' I thought about his bookshelves, the battered puzzle books I'd seen. 'Everyone's got to have a hobby, I guess. And aside from that and his garden, I don't know what else he does with his time.'

I downed the last of the Coke. Stood up. 'Thanks,' I said. 'You've been a big help.'

'Right,' he said. 'You ever write a book about this, be sure and send one for Mo. She'd love it, you know?'

'I'll remember that.'

ELEVEN

Leaving the pub, I felt at a loss.

What the hell was I doing here? Reopening an old man's wounds because of a hunch?

Or worse, was I distracting myself from real problems? Such as Griggs's attempts to manipulate me?

I took a walk down to the river, walked the footpath like any other tourist. It was late in the day. I'd wound up hanging around longer than anticipated. Talking to Moorehead's father had left me feeling restless, uncertain. The drive back seemed long and daunting. Four hours could be an eternity in the wrong frame of mind. What I needed was to unwind. To digest everything I had heard. I thought about the call of a pint at the Coleman Arms. The appeal of a freshly laundered hotel bed.

Maybe it would be a good idea. Give me time to rest and reassess.

More important, give me a chance to have that pint. Some things in life can always be eased by a good beer.

Walking the river, the chirping of crickets

erupted from somewhere nearby, along with the call of birds somewhere among the trees. The sounds were unfamiliar to me. Dundee is hardly a metropolis, but its sounds are those of industry and the modern age: the rush of cars, the hum of generators, the beat of music from clubs and pubs. Those were the noises that welcomed my nights. To hear the sounds of animals and the rush of water was unsettling. And, at the same time, relaxing. I closed my eyes as I stood at the edge of the river and just let it wash over me.

My phone vibrated gently.

I took a deep breath. Even out here, in a place that promised isolation and calm, there was always something to remind you that society wasn't ready to let you go. There is always a reminder; a message, an alert, a vibration that recalls you to your duties in the twenty-four-hour, never-sleep culture that we have slowly established since the industrial revolution. You could never really escape. Tied by invisible cords to the rest of your life, no matter where you ran to.

I checked the display that glowed unnaturally in the dim light of early evening. Unknown number. Clicked to the message content.

Any thoughts? Offer won't last forever. S.

I nearly tossed the phone. Just wanted rid of it. And the rest of my life. Had this urge to run into the trees across the other side of the water. Return to nature completely. Forget about the world, about all the expectations that civilization brought with it.

But I didn't.

What I did was, I pocketed my phone, turned and walked back to the village.

I woke at 3 a.m., swallowed, still tasting the whisky I'd taken as a nightcap at the bar. The bartender had brought through Mo, his wife, so they could talk to me about what it meant to be a real private detective. They were hospitable and attentive, but all I really wanted was to get to my room and get my head together. By the time I was on my third Talisker, I persuaded them that I needed to do some paperwork before retiring.

Truth be told, though, I could feel myself getting drunk, reaching the point of no return. And I wanted my head clear in the morning.

The room they gave me was small, tucked away on the second floor, at the rear of the building. There were wooden struts built into the whitewashed walls. It was the kind of room Sherlock Holmes might have taken when a case required a country visit. The bed welcomed me with a comforting but firm embrace, and I was gone the moment my head hit the pillow. No time to undress or get under the sheets.

★ ★ ★

But then, at 3 a.m., I woke.

My eyes adjusted to the gloom. Something tickled at the back of my mind, maybe the remnants of a dream, or some idea that had been struggling to form while I slept. I tried to let it come through, take on some shape I could recognize, but nothing happened.

Eventually I gave in and tried to close my eyes.

But I couldn't relax.

I swung my legs off the bed. Finally, I took off my shoes and let my bare feet sink into the thick carpet. Stood up, walked to the window, looked out across the car park and to the countryside beyond. I understood why Jonathan Moorehead would choose a place like this. There was nowhere he could hide without the risk of someone like Mo recognizing his face, making the connection to the man he was trying to hide from. But at least in a place like this, he could pretend that the rest of the world no longer existed. Lose himself in the illusion of isolation. City workers escaped the reality of their working life by retreating to the countryside. A man like Jonathan Moorehead could attempt the same thing.

I wondered if it worked. Had my visit brought back unpleasant memories he had laid to rest? Or did he still live with them every day, unable to escape no matter how hard he tried?

7.30 found me awake once more. I had spent maybe half an hour feeling like I'd never sleep again, before it took me without warning. But when I opened my eyes, that itch was still at the back of my brain; an idea I couldn't quite express, that insisted upon itself but had no idea how to achieve comprehensibility.

I showered, got dressed in the clothes I'd worn the day before. Not much I could do about that, considering I hadn't planned on staying overnight. I didn't think it was too noticeable, however. When I figured I was presentable, I slipped downstairs where the bartender and his wife had assured me there would be a full breakfast laid on.

At nine, I walked to the newsagent's. The village was waking up, but I couldn't see any difference from the evening before, when I first arrived. A few more people on the streets perhaps, none of them paying attention to me, probably used to tourists and visitors in the area.

The bell jangled above my head as I entered the tiny shop. How much of this, I had to wonder, was for show? The village seemed like an actor who never left his role, who was always in character.

There were only three of us in the store. Myself, the woman behind the till, and Jonathan Moorehead. He had his back to me, paying for his paper. I pretended to examine the racks until he turned around.

'I thought you were gone,' he said.

'Please, just hear me out.'

We walked down to the water's edge. The sun hid behind the clouds, and the air was a little frosty. 'Always starts cold, even in summer,' Mr Moorehead said. 'Warms up by eleven, usually.'

We didn't say much more for a while.

I let him set the pace.

'Why are you here?'

'You never talked to your son,' I said. 'Even when we asked for your assistance.'

'What was I supposed to say?'

'He might have listened to you. You're his father.'

'Would you still listen to your dad?'

'Yes,' I said. 'We all would. Our parents...' I hesitated. 'They have power over us, whether we admit it or not.'

'I don't have power over him. If I did, then he wouldn't be where he is now. Nothing's changed since you last tried to talk me round to this.'

'He wasn't ready to talk before,' I said. 'He might be, now. With the right persuasion.'

'What good would it do?'

'If he could tell us about the other bodies,' I said, 'it would lay a lot of ghosts to rest.'

Mr Moorehead seemed to consider this for

a moment. He picked up a stone from the bank, skimmed it across the water to the other side. 'When he was a boy, he loved to skim stones. We'd go walking, find a river or a small pond, bounce those pebbles as far as we could. Even better, when we went to the beach.'

'I know it's a lot to ask,' I said. 'But it would help my client lay her own ghosts to rest. Maybe others, too.'

He considered this. Then said, 'I'll need some time. To think it over.'

TWELVE

I was back in Dundee that afternoon. Sorted some paperwork before calling Mrs Farnham.

Displacement activity? She had asked that I update her every two to three days, even if there was nothing much to say. And I felt there was nothing much to say right now. She just wanted to know that I was working the case.

I've never been comfortable with clients who want close contact. Always feels like they don't quite trust you.

They probably don't.

'Nothing's changed for his father,' I said. 'Same as it was. He doesn't want anything to do with his son. Doesn't want to face the possibility that he was in some way responsible for what happened.'

'Every parent feels responsible for their child's behaviour.' She paused for a moment. 'I remember when I'd get the call from the school, you know, if Justin misbehaved. I'd wonder what I'd done as a parent to make him act like that. The guilt...' I could hear a small smile in her voice, laughing at herself and her own foolishness as if she couldn't quite connect the memories to the very real tragedy that was to follow them. '...the guilt was overwhelming to me. Second-guessing the values I taught him, the way I treated him. I can only imagine how Mr Moorehead feels...'

Her thoughts trailed off. I had nothing to fill the empty air between us.

Finally, she said, 'I'd like to meet him.'

'I don't think that's a good idea.'

She was silent. Had I insulted her? 'I just want him to take this slowly. In many ways he's tried to distance himself from what happened. If anything were to push him away again, even accidentally.'

'Of course,' she said. 'I understand.'

But there was a disappointment in her voice. She didn't really understand. Even though she knew it was a bad idea, she thought I wasn't pushing sufficiently.

Maybe I wasn't.

I wanted to help her. No question about that. But I didn't want to dredge up this old case again. All those years ago, Ernie had been convinced the right man paid the price for murdering Elizabeth Farnham's son. The investigation had been long and tiring.

I had thought to myself when it was over that at least this monster was behind bars. At least he was paying for what he had done.

There was justice in that. For Elizabeth Farnham. For her son. And later, I'd realize, for a lot of other parents whose children had met this bastard, this near-silent psychopath who refused to acknowledge the cost of his actions.

I said, 'I'll find another way.'

'I know you will.'

When I was finished with the call, I pulled out my mobile and looked at the message from Sandy again.

Read it three times. Then deleted it completely.

Fuck him.

'I try not to judge people, even those my fellow officers tell me are utter pricks.' Wemyss, on the other end of the line, was trying to remain calm. I could picture him sitting at his desk, knuckles white from gripping the receiver, round face cherry red. Heart probably working overtime, too. 'But the fact is, McNee, you're every bit as much of an arse as your reputation suggests.'

'You want an end to this operation as much as I do.'

'The father fucking hates him, McNee. He did then, and I see no reason why that's changed just because you've whispered a few sweet nothings into his ancient lugholes.'

'He didn't do it before because everything he did then was under media surveillance.

He was judged every time he took a breath. That kind of scrutiny can paralyse a person, make them doubt what they're doing. Even if what they're doing is the right thing. He couldn't have taken a shite without the red tops wondering what it all meant. He wanted to put as much distance between himself and his son as he could. And he didn't see why he needed to help us, because as far as he was concerned, we had our man and could do what the fuck we liked with him.'

'I know you think you're doing the right thing, McNee. But Mrs Farnham, she's cracked. You know that as well as me. You've talked to her. The years haven't been kind. She's round the bend. It was always going to happen. And what really makes me sick is that a parasite like you is taking her money. When you know better than anyone what she went through.'

'If it wasn't me, it would be someone else. I never promised her the answers she wanted. I promised her that I would do my best. That one way or the other I would try to see if her own suspicions had any basis in reality. She's not cracked. She's confused. As anyone would be. I'm doing this because I remember what the death of her son did to her, and I want her to finally have some sense of closure. I'm doing this to help her.'

'Jesus! You sound like you believe your own hype.'

'Believe what you like, Wemyss.'

'If he comes forward, I'll let him talk to his son. But don't think you're getting any credit. Word's spreading, McNee. Bad enough you managed to get one of our own falsely accused of perverting justice, but now it's sounding to me like you've got a real history. Lock the doors, pal. They're coming for you.'

He was talking about the charges. The ones that Griggs had re-opened. Looked like my friends at the SCDEA were willing to make my life difficult until I did what they wanted. A little friendly extortion among professionals never hurt anyone.

Made me wonder how desperate Griggs was.

Whether his own job was hanging in the balance.

When Wemyss hung up, I held the receiver for a few moments, listened to the tone.

I was physically exhausted. The reminder of the charges I was facing had made me nauseous.

In the back of my mind, there was the worry that maybe I had done something wrong, that there really was a better choice I could have made that evening.

I went to the bathroom, splashed my face with cold water. A slap in the face, enough to make me focus. Looking at myself in the mirror, I wondered what I would do if they made the charges official. Was there any way to deny what had happened?

I had done the right thing that night. I knew that in my heart. Would stand by my actions. Wouldn't change a thing. The two men in the Necropolis all those years ago had been killers. Their history spoke volumes. I had seen their handiwork close up only a few days before I killed one of them. They deserved everything they got.

Sometimes there is a difference between justice and due process. At the time, I'd figured that perhaps the universe realized that, too. That I'd got a lucky break. Karma, perhaps. The kind of thing you consider even if you don't believe, because it makes you feel good to impose that kind of narrative on events.

But you can't kill someone – no matter how honourable your intentions – and expect nothing to happen.

I heard a buzz from my office. I dried my face with the hand towel, hit the intercom button. Dot said, 'There's a Detective Sergeant Kellen to see you.'

I opened the door to reception. DS Kellen stood by Dot's desk. Kellen was in her late thirties, with a severe face and blonde hair scraped back from her forehead. Off duty, she could have been attractive. But it was hard to tell when she wore her professional attitude like the uniform she'd once worn on the beat.

She came over to me, didn't offer her hand. 'Mr McNee,' she said. 'We need to talk.'

'About?'

'I think you know.'

Was this the moment I had been dreading? I let her in to my office. Closed the door.

THIRTEEN

'Are there official charges to be made?'

'I'm not here to arrest you.'

'Good.'

'I don't think you pose a flight risk.'

'Good.'

'I do think you're guilty.'

There was no response to that.

'I've been looking at your history. Good cop. Bright future. Could have been running CID by now, maybe taking a shot at a more political role.'

Kellen kept looking at me, as though to check that she was getting through, making her point. She knew me on paper, but any good cop will tell you that a file only tells partial stories. How you get a feel for someone, it's all about the way they react when you have them across the table. 'But that's not your style. Never was. You were "hands on", right? It's OK, I understand. You like to feel you're making a difference. Hard to do that when all you see are reports and numbers and statistics.'

'Some people do just fine.'

'Not people like you.' She was testing the waters. Seeing how I reacted to what she said. 'I've read the reports on your departure from the force. You blamed yourself as much as you blamed DI Lindsay.' She hesitated. 'How is he, by the way? I believe the two of you are talking again?'

I didn't give her a response.

'Doesn't matter,' she said. 'I'll be calling on him later. He wrote the initial report on the shooting incident. Given your ... antagonistic ... relationship, I think he was generous regarding your involvement. And your motives.'

I wondered how much she really knew. My sessions with the psychologist – the ones I'd been forced to attend after the accident – were confidential; a way of helping me cope with what had happened. But she was making it sound like she knew what was in the man's files. A good trick, of course. One I'd used myself. It was easy to make assumptions if you had any idea about how human psychology worked, no matter how broadly. It's the same kind of trickery that so-called psychics use to convince people they're speaking to dead friends and relatives.

But I knew the tricks.

Wasn't about to give her anything.

All the same, I had to ask: 'Did you know Kevin Wood?'

She shook her head. 'I transferred in after

... the incident.'

'The incident?' I tried not to laugh. In-nuendo gets me that way. Her way of not mentioning that the man who had nearly been put in charge of Tayside Police had been a drug-dealing scumbag who hung a decent copper out to dry. You wanted to investigate someone's past cases, why not look at his? Because no one really wanted him to be the bad guy, no matter how strong the evidence was. And while no one could deny the truth, they could at least not talk about it.

Complicity through silence?

Denial, certainly.

And who could blame anyone for doing that? The thing about being a copper is the sense of family. If one of us lets the side down, we feel like everyone has. Our first instinct is to back each other up.

Kellen regarded me for a moment. Her eyes were perfectly still. The frozen-over surface of a river in winter. 'There is no conspiracy here, Mr McNee. No one looking to get revenge over you taking down one of our own. Truth be told, if you were anyone else, I think they'd be celebrating what you did. But when you add what happened to the long list of your fuck-ups? Well, I can see why you'd be paranoid.'

There was no deception in the way she spoke. Her body language was formal but relaxed. She had nothing to hide from me. She was here out of professional courtesy. Like touching gloves before the opening round of a boxing match.

'This is an informal chat, Mr McNee. We'll be bringing charges against you. One way or the other.'

'Then do it,' I said.

'Where did you get the gun?'

'What gun?'

'The third gun.'

'You read the report. One of them had a second weapon.'

'How did you get hold of it?'

'It was four years ago. I can barely remember what I had for breakfast today.'

'Your memory isn't good. You fudged your story even on the night of the incident. There are one or two things that just didn't add up.'

'I was in a stressful situation. Frightened for my life.'

'And the lives of others?'

'My client.'

'Mr James Robertson. Who tried to kill himself a few days later.'

'Because of the guilt he felt over killing his own brother.'

'Yes.' She took a deep breath. Her eyes remained focused on me. Waiting for the tell; that moment of weakness she could exploit.

'You were a professional witness at James Robertson's trial.'

'Yes.'

'You confronted him over the matter of his brother's murder shortly before he tried to kill himself.'

'Yes.'

'Yet you never came forward until after Mr Robertson attempted to kill himself?'

I had been a different person then. My own anger had burned hard and fierce. I was looking for destruction. If not my own, then someone else's. When I confronted Robertson about his brother's death, I made it clear that the best option he had was to take his own life.

No one would be sorry.

Except the attempt went horribly wrong.

I remember seeing Robertson in court, confined to a wheelchair for the rest of his life. A deep shame had built in my chest; a blockage that threatened to choke me. It was the first time I realized the absolute consequences of my own actions.

Or inactions.

'I figured he'd do the right thing. I wasn't a copper then. I couldn't arrest him.'

'You figured he'd do the right thing? Can you tell me what the right thing would have been?'

'To turn himself in, admit his complicity in the death of his brother.'

Even now, the lie came easily. Enough I could have believed it was the honest truth.

'That's what you were thinking?'

'That's what I remember. It was a bad judgement call, yes. But you can hardly—'

'You're a good liar, Mr McNee.'

I didn't rise to that one. No point. Would only have weakened my position. But I was exposed and vulnerable. She wasn't going to give me a chance. DS Kellen was after my blood.

I don't know why. We'd never met before. Figured she must be a new transfer. Maybe trying to prove herself. But she'd hinted earlier at her opinion of me. On paper, I probably looked like a bastard. My involvement in at least three high-profile cases over the last few years, and unanswered questions about my motivations and actions, would have raised my own doubts if I'd been charged to investigate them.

But the timing was bad. Kellen coming after me so hard made Griggs's offer that much more appealing. If I was going down, it'd be wise to take the soft route and use all of this to my advantage.

Kellen had called me paranoid earlier. Maybe I was. I don't doubt that Griggs planned this; opening the file in the first place to try and smoke me out. I wondered if he knew it would land on Kellen's desk. Did they know each other? Or did he just decide she would be the right person for the job?

I'd be lying if I said I wasn't slightly tempted by Griggs's offer. Taking down Burns would not only be a personal achievement, but it would honour the now tainted memory of my friend and mentor, Ernie Bright.

But I didn't want to do it like this.

'Is there anything else?' I was calm and composed on the outside.

Kellen smiled, lips pressed tight together. She shook her head. 'Just getting to know you, McNee. Trying to clear up a few details is all.'

'When can I expect to hear from you?'

'Soon,' she said. 'So if there's anything you need to do. To prepare, I mean. Then I'd do it fast.'

She stood up. I mirrored her, and then offered my hand.

She didn't take it.

I never expected her to.

I spent the next hour composing an email to Susan.

Explaining to her what had happened.

Telling her that I missed her.

The mail was long, heartfelt, rambling and honest. The most honest I'd been with myself or anyone else in a long time. I read it over again, hovered the mouse over the 'send' button, before my hand slipped and I sent all of those words to the wastebasket. I deleted the message permanently. No more temptation.

What the hell use was there in sending that email?

What could Susan do halfway across the world, still dealing with her own problems?

FOURTEEN

'Mr McNee?'

I recognized the voice on the other end of the line. Jonathan Moorehead. Sounding uncertain, hesitant even.

It was eight o'clock. I was settling in with a takeout I'd grabbed from Beiderbeckes on the way home. I could smell the coconut-infused sauce before I even opened the container.

'Mr Moorehead,' I said. 'It's good to hear from you.'

'Not good to be calling you. I called the fat bugger in charge of the investigation. He doesn't like you too much.'

'I have that effect on people.'

'I gathered. That why you're no longer police?'

'That and a few other things.'

'He talked me round. I didn't tell him you had a small part in that. But figured you'd like to know.'

'I'm glad,' I said.

'If it wasn't for you,' he said, 'none of this would have happened. No, that's not true. If it wasn't for your client ... I'd like to meet her ... to...'

'No,' I said. 'Client confidentiality. I can't...'

'Of course,' he said. 'Of course. I do hope that this brings her answers. And peace.'

There was an edge to his voice. Maybe he didn't quite believe what he was saying. Battling second thoughts and guesses.

It was three days.

Three days before the phone rang again and I heard Wemyss's voice on the other end of the line.

'Fuck you, Dr Freud.'

I couldn't figure what was happening. It was 6 a.m. and I wasn't quite awake yet.

'Fuck you, Dr Freud,' he said again, each word cold and clear. 'What is it with you? Are you jinxed?'

I couldn't follow what he was saying.

'Alex Moorehead is dead,' he said. 'And it's all your fucking fault, you sanctimonious wee bawbag.'

I met him at the same place we'd had breakfast a few weeks earlier. Despite the bad news, his appetite was unaffected. All I could do was look at my bacon roll and feel nauseous.

'Hung himself with bed sheets. Dead before we had a chance to do anything. All these years, he's never been on suicide watch. Living in absolute solitary. Happy enough that way, too. Aye, and then you finally persuade dear old Dad to visit...'

'So what happened?'

'They talked.'

'About?'

'What the fuck do you think?'

'Did it affect him, I mean, at the time?'

Wemyss laughed. 'What do you think?'

'Did he show outward signs? Of being affected? Of anything?'

'What do you care?'

'Why'd you ask me here?'

He sighed. 'I did some digging. Old pal of mine was the one vouched for you. Said that you were a pain in the arse, but you could get results. And that you usually knew more than you let on.'

I couldn't think of anyone who'd say that about me on the force. Not these days.

'Know who it was? Know why I took them at their word?'

I shook my head.

'George Lindsay. He's your guardian bastard angel.'

I wanted to laugh. Covered it by sipping at my sour-tasting coffee.

'Most other people told me that you only fucked things up. Have to say, right now, I'm thinking they were right. And that George's head had been all fucked up by being in that coma. Aye, the one you helped him get into.'

I wondered why he asked me here.

'You talked to the father,' Wemyss said. 'Persuaded him to have a wee chat with Alex. After all these years, all it took was one visit from you and Dad's suddenly ready to reach a reconciliation.'

'I don't think that was me.'

'Then tell me, McNee, what the fuck was it? What changed?'

'I wish I could tell you.'

I really did. When I first showed up at Jonathan Moorehead's door, he'd been un-willing to talk. No danger he'd even embrace the idea of opening those old wounds. And then suddenly he was dashing up north for a father and son reunion. That ended with the death of his son.

Aye, it seemed odd right enough.

But then the case had always felt odd to me. Even back at the beginning, I'd had my doubts. Only I hadn't really expressed them, still looking up at my senior officer with the kind of starry-eyed hero-worship normally reserved for awestruck teens. I couldn't con-tradict him. He knew what he was talking about. I, on the other hand, was still learn-ing.

What would have happened if I'd held my ground?

'I didn't do anything special,' I said. 'Be-yond appealing to Moorehead's father to do the right thing.'

'Did you tell him about your client?'

'As much as I told you.'

'I know who your client was.'

'You'd be dumb if you didn't work it out. But Moorehead senior wouldn't have a reason to figure out who it was. There's a long list to work through.'

There was silence for a moment. Around us, the world continued. People's lives stepped forward at the same pace they always did.

But for us, there was a moment. A second.

One where we realized that our lives were on the same trajectory, heading in the same direction. We were locked together.

It wasn't fate. It was who we were.

Wemyss was a good cop. He wanted answers. More than that, he wanted the world to order itself according to principles that most people would agree were fair and just.

And I was simply a stubborn bastard.

Wemyss said, 'Right. Fair enough. I want you to look at the tape, McNee.'

'Why?'

'Just look. Tell me what you see. Prove to me that that old bugger Lindsay isn't losing his mind by saying I could trust you.'

FIFTEEN

Watch enough TV, you might think that the world is filled with technology; smartphones, flat screens, hi-def, LED, LCD, HDMI magic. The guys on *CSI* might as well be working on the bridge of the USS *Enterprise*.

But in the places where such technology might matter, you find that the world is not quite where we're led to believe it's at. While the public drool and salivate over increasingly sophisticated technology, and believe that behind closed doors all the government and authority figures have even cooler toys, the truth is that what you see in the gleaming police stations on your flat-screen 40inch is pure fantasy. *CSI* never has to deal with budget cuts, backlogs, cost-cutting and red tape.

Which is why I was in a room that looked like it hadn't seen a fresh coat of paint since the late seventies, watching a grainy video feed on a great big grey box that had never known what the future would bring and could barely spell HD if you gave it a subscription to Sky One.

The telly was wheeled in from another room. It was likely it was the only one in the building. Maybe they'd sold the rest to pay for dry-cleaning uniforms. With the current government, you never could tell.

I sat forward on the foldaway. The screen became my world. Overhead angle, high corner of the room. As per the agreements reached after hours of negotiations with both parties, there was no sound, no one else in the room. It was the only way Alex would agree to talk with his father.

They sat at opposite sides of the table. Someone had observed the video feed the whole time. If they got too close, moved around the table, or even attempted to touch, the interview was over. This was Wemyss's part of the bargain. He was already taking a chance. He wanted them to know that he wasn't going to suffer either party taking advantage of the situation.

Either Jonathan Moorehead had taken Wemyss's warnings seriously, or his intentions were exactly as advertised. Because he obeyed the rules at all times. When he entered the room, he hesitated with the door still open, and for a moment it looked as though he was ready to turn on his heels and get the fuck out of there. An understandable reaction. It's easy to believe you can go through with something right up until the moment it becomes real. He had not seen his son since the trial. He'd only been able to come to any kind of terms with Alex's crimes because it's easy to push something out of your head when you don't have to see a reminder of it every day.

But when he walked into that room, you saw it in his posture. The video may have been grainy, the frame-rate poor so that you felt like the action was jumping rather than flowing smoothly, but Jonathan Moorehead's body-language played to the back row. He saw his son, and it was like someone wired him up to the mains.

After he sat down, the two men said nothing for a long time. They simply looked at each other across the table.

At first it seemed like Alex was relaxed. At least, more than his father. He sat back in his chair, where good old Dad leaned forward.

It was Dad did all the talking. All the gesturing.

Alex remained sitting back in his chair.

But a closer look, and I realized he wasn't relaxed. This wasn't a killer playing it cool or some late-blooming attempt at the kind of rebellion only teenagers can muster.

This was fear.

He was stiff. Sitting back as far as he could to escape the older man's judgement. That was why he wasn't moving. He had nowhere to go.

I paused the video. Stood up. Paced.

Thinking that I was reading things into the images that might not be there. As though Elizabeth Farnham's absolute belief in her son's killer's innocence was infectious.

I was looking for evidence of his innocence. Grabbing at the smallest signs I could. Almost desperate to find something.

Perhaps because I believed his suicide told me something I didn't know before.

Innocent men kill themselves the same as guilty men. Maybe more so.

Alex Moorehead told us he had killed Justin Farnham. He admitted it in a moment of intensity that stood at odds with his later calm.

But what if he had lied?

What if he took the crime on his shoulders for other reasons?

After a few minutes of pacing, clearing my brain, I sat down again on the folding chair, watched the rest of the conversation. After several minutes of Dad talking, it was Alex's turn. He spoke, facing away from his dad, like he couldn't look the other man in the eyes. Still that whole sulky teenager vibe to the way he sat and the way he communicated. A completely different person to the one I'd talked to only a few days earlier.

When Alex's father left the room, the timer read 19.20.

Nineteen minutes. Twenty seconds.

And a few hours later, Alex Moorehead

would be dead, his father missing. A new mystery, one more frustrating than the one that preceded it, because this time there was no one left who could give us the answers.

'Well?'

'It's hard to say.'

'You see the point where he snapped?'

We were in the incident room. Drinking weak coffee from polystyrene cups. The Mothers of the Disappeared – and the Disappeared themselves – stared from their assigned places on the pinboards and wall space.

'The second he saw his father,' I said. 'It's subtle, but it's there. I thought he was relaxed. I thought he was cool. But he was petrified.'

'Strange, isn't it?' Wemyss said. 'That the old man spends all these years avoiding his son and yet he's here like a shot when someone suggests the possibility of Alex's innocence.'

'Maybe we finally gave him hope?'

'I talked to him,' Wemyss said. 'Before I put them in the room. The old man didn't believe in his son's innocence. That wasn't why he was here.'

'Then why?'

Wemyss stayed quiet.

I could figure it out. It wasn't hard to see what had happened. During their discussion, Jonathan Moorehead had convinced his son to take his own life.

The question then became, why?

Is this what he had been waiting for? Is this why he came all this way? Thinking maybe if he got his son to kill himself, then he wouldn't have to do it himself? Could clear himself of any guilt?

'Have you talked to Jonathan Moorehead since Alex's death?' I asked.

Wemyss shook his head. 'By the time we found out what had happened, he was checked out of his hotel. On his way back down to the border. At least I assume that's where he was heading.'

'You've tried calling him?'

Wemyss bristled. Looked ready to lamp me one. I couldn't really blame him. I was here because he asked me, and now I was questioning his professional competence.

So I answered my own question. 'You tried and he didn't answer.'

'Nothing from the mobile or the landline. There's a couple of local lads down that way owe me a favour. They've been waiting for hours now. No sign of him. The journey from here to Moorehead's house only takes about four hours if you know what you're doing.'

'So where is he?'

'Fucked if I know.' Wemyss hesitated. He was tense, and I knew he wanted to lash out.

All that energy buzzing just beneath his skin, the muscles trembling, the heart tripping to its own beat.

'Are you glad he's dead?' Meaning Alex.

'No. The prick took innocent children with him. We'll never find their bodies.'

But an unanswered sentence was left unsaid. *If he even killed those kids in the first place.*

SIXTEEN

Back in the days when everything was simple, when the world made sense, Ernie Bright was everything I wanted to be. He had seen policing at its best and worst, coming through the other side with a strong sense of morality, highly attuned to the realities of the world.

Even if I had managed to partially redeem his memory, there were still unanswered questions about his actual loyalties. I had found a paper trail that led from his bank account to the laundered money of one of Dundee's biggest criminals. And I still didn't understand why. What was their relationship? Who was Ernie Bright to David Burns?

But back in the good old days, none of that mattered.

We used to drink at the Phoenix on the Perth Road. Not a copper's boozer, but more a second home for its regulars, who came from all walks of life. Back in those days, the landlord used to be behind the bar every time we walked in; a larger than life figure who liked to try and have a bit of fun with his punters.

'What can I get you, gents?'

I was on the Deuchars, but Ernie wasn't willing to get more than a Coke, which earned him a ribbing. Truth was, he'd done his back in chasing a suspect who decided he didn't want to be interviewed. Ernie liked to keep his head on straight, and the idea of mixing painkillers and alcohol wasn't one that filled him with joy. Mind you, when we retired to one of the corners, he said it might have been better than putting up with the landlord's jokes.

'You wanted to talk?'

'Aye,' I said. Feeling daft, like this whole chat was a bad idea.

But we were here, and the drinks were down.

'You know about the Young case?'

'Young? Oh, you mean the perv?'

'That's the one.'

The case had been open for months. Aaron Young had been making perverted calls to women around the city. I knew the copper who brought him in. Name of Parker. We'd worked together a few times. I didn't have strong feelings about him as a copper. He did the job, said the right things to the right people, didn't make waves. Thing was, I knew the call that Parker charged Young with was not one that Young had made.

And Parker knew that, too.

But what do you do?

Dob in a fellow officer? People joke about the thin blue line, but those who walk along it understand how sometimes there can be temptations to bend the rules.

Ernie wasn't a squealer. Wasn't going to run to internal affairs. While the blue line maybe isn't as thick as some would like you to believe, it still exists. Where we can, we still try to protect our own.

So I told him.

Keeping names out of it.

Just in case.

'I'm not reporting anyone,' Ernie said. 'But I've considered it myself more than once. It's the best solution to a bad problem. You fit someone up not because they did it but because they might as well have done it, or because they're the easy solution to your problem.'

'We did it because we knew about the other—'

'Are you going to justify this to me?'

'No.'

He nodded. 'It's a choice you have to make yourself. But I've often thought about what would be the worst thing that could happen to me as a copper. I came to the conclusion that it would be making sure a jury sent the wrong guy away. And knowing that I'd done it.'

'And what if the wrong guy was still a

scumbag?'

'Doesn't matter. He's innocent of that one crime, then he doesn't deserve to pay for it. Get him for what he did do.'

I thought it over. Sipped my pint slowly.

I trusted Ernie. Believed what he told me. He was a good copper. The model I aspired to.

And even years later, given all that I learned about his past and his relationship with David Burns, and all the questions that hung in the air over his death, I still lived by the advice he had given me.

If he's innocent, he doesn't deserve to pay for it.

If there was any doubt in my mind about Alex Moorehead's guilt or innocence, I had to confirm whether that doubt was justified. Because even if he'd done bad things in his life, the idea that he had served a sentence for something he hadn't done was never going to sit easy with me.

And it wouldn't sit well with Ernie, either.

SEVENTEEN

Three days.

No sign of Moorehead senior. Like he'd vanished.

The Great Houdini.

Last time anyone saw him was as he left the prison. He didn't say anything, just walked to his car, started the engine and drove away.

I was out of the loop, officially speaking. Wemyss had called me in just to show me how badly I'd fucked up the case. Now he was pursuing his own lines of inquiry.

I knew what he was thinking: the father had something to hide. Something that his son had said or that he had said to his son. Something none of us ever got to hear. Something you couldn't even try and lip-read. The angle was wrong, and the picture too grainy to make out the finer details.

All the same, it seemed obvious. If we were stuck in some cheap thriller, the dad would be the bad guy and soon enough the hero cop would track him down and get him to confess. That's how these things worked. That's how we expected them to work.

Nothing to say that wasn't going to happen. But I figured there was more going on than that.

Because what I've found is that in real life there is usually no such thing as the simple explanation. The further back you go trying to explain something, the more tied up in knots the narrative becomes. You can't untangle motivation and action into a neat and explicable line. There are always loose ends, doubts and unanswered questions. Events rarely turn out the way you expect them to.

And you don't always see them tied up and delivered with a bow. Sometimes gaffer tape, perhaps, but never a bow.

Mrs Farnham's deposits came through as she told me they would, along with an email thanking me for all I had done.

Question was, had I really done anything? Was she merely fulfilling her obligation as a client? Or merely happy for any kind of closure? After all, with Alex Moorehead dead, she could tell herself anything she liked. And it had to be true because no one else could tell her different.

Now all I had left was waiting for the other shoe to drop regarding my suspension from the Association and the charges that Sandy Griggs had threatened me with.

DI Kellen hadn't made her move yet.

Made me wonder what she was waiting for. Permission? Or the kind of evidence that would damn me no matter what I said?

I distracted myself with paperwork. Found that I kept thinking about Alex Moorehead. About the reasons why he would kill himself.

If it was guilt, and if he felt that guilt so deeply that he took his own life, then why did he wait so long to do it?

What changed?

Elizabeth Farnham lived just north of Camperdown, on the edge of the city. Isolated enough, and perhaps a reminder of her days when she lived with her husband and son in the country. Before her son was taken from her. Before her husband left to deal with their loss in his own way. Before her world was destroyed.

As I pulled up outside the modest bungalow, I noticed a number of cars parked on the street outside. I had to pull in maybe fifteen, twenty metres away and walk back down. The air was cool, but not unpleasant, and the wind ruffled, caressing me.

I thought about Susan. But only for a moment.

As I got to the front door, I saw into the living room through the large windows at the front. There were people gathered in there. All of them sitting around, talking. Like a book group or a community meeting, perhaps.

I wanted to turn and go. But someone had

already seen me.

Elizabeth Farnham was on her feet, looking out at me.

We met at the front door, where she kept her distance from me.

'I'm sorry,' I said. 'I didn't know...'

'Why are you here?'

'I wanted to apologize. I just ... what you asked me to do ... I know that it wasn't...'

'You did everything you could.'

'I didn't do anything.'

She didn't reply.

I said, 'I should go.' Wondering what impulse had made me come out here in the first place.

'No,' she said. Looking at me oddly, a hesitance and an uncertainty about her that I'd seen before, when she first asked for my help. 'Come in,' she said, finally. 'I think you should meet the rest of us.'

It was a room full of ghosts.

When I walked in, everyone's eyes fell on me. I was an intruder in their space. Their gaze was expectant; as though they expected me to bring answers they had been seeking all their life.

And these women were seeking answers.

The same answers Mrs Farnham wanted.

As I looked around the room, I knew every face there. Had seen all of them in the past few days, staring from the walls of a police incident room. But in that room, they had been lifeless; frozen in a moment, rendered unreal by the magic of photography.

Now they were in front of me, brought to life, and the sadness I felt looking at them only increased with their newfound reality.

I wanted to tell them how sorry I was for what had happened, how I wished I could tell them the truth, finally let them come to terms with the deaths of their sons.

But I couldn't.

All I could do was stand there.

One of the women finally spoke out. I recognized her. Older than the image I had seen, but still with the same eyes and pointed chin that made her face seem severe up until the moment she smiled. Her name was Mary Warrington, and her son's name had been Kyle. 'You spoke to him. Alex Moorehead. Elizabeth says you were the last person to speak to him before...'

'I wish he had told me something.'

Another woman spoke. More hesitant, her words coming out in bursts, like she had to breathe between each syllable. She was older than the rest, had allowed her hair to grey and her skin to sag, accepting the inevitability of her years. No longer a mother, she could have been a grandmother. It took me a moment to place her face on the wall, to know her name. 'You looked into his eyes. Tell me, did he do it? Did he kill our sons?'

The question demanded an answer. A definitive one.

I had avoided giving one up until now, even to myself.

'I think...' I hesitated. They were watching me, all of them. None of them moving. As frozen as their photographs. 'I don't know. But I want to find the answers.'

I felt a ripple run through them. Like a crowd of lions who'd just realized how hungry they were.

The woman whose voice had cracked spoke up again, stronger this time. 'We've heard empty promises before, Mr McNee.'

Someone else said, 'You were the one who made them. You and your detective inspector.'

'I'm not making promises,' I said. 'I'm not asking for money. But you deserve answers, and I think that Alex Moorehead's death has opened up lines of inquiry that may have been hidden before.'

'But you will want money?'

'No,' I said. 'No money. This is for you. For your sons. Maybe too little, too late. But it's something.'

'If you want to help us,' Mrs Farnham said, 'then maybe you should stay. Just for a little while.' She gestured for me to take a seat.

I hesitated.

But then stepped forward, sat down.

And listened.

EIGHTEEN

I could not bring back their sons.

Their boys were gone for ever.

But I could offer them closure.

It's one thing to realize that you can't save everybody, that you can't solve every problem. It's another thing to quit trying.

Old habits. Hard to quit.

This one was harder than smoking.

I used to use it as an excuse to escape from myself. Lose myself in other people's problems to try and deflect the reality of my own life. Two years earlier, I'd doggedly pursued a missing teenager not because anyone asked me to but because it stopped me from thinking about how much of a mess my own life was in at the time.

I'd wound up making things worse, of course.

Because I wasn't focused.

Because I was escaping something else.

He was waiting for me. Sitting out in reception and chatting to Dot. Smiled when I came in, and I thought of a wolf from some

Grimm Brothers' fairy tale.

The Sandy Griggs I remembered was a decent guy. Hell of a temper, sure, but one of the good ones. Now it was like something else had slipped into that man's skin. It leered out at me from beneath the exterior of the placid policeman.

I felt like Little Red Riding Hood seeing her grandma on that blood-soaked morning.

'I don't have the time,' I told him. He didn't get the message.

In my office, the door closed, I said, 'Make your charges or get the hell out of my life.' The waiting made it worse. A fact he was more than aware of. Something, I'm sure, he was counting on.

He pulled an envelope from the inside pocket of his jacket and passed it to me. I took it reluctantly and looked inside.

'Recognize her?'

The image was fifteen or twenty years earlier, but just three hours ago I'd sat in a room with this woman and listened to her tell me about the pain her son's disappearance had caused her, how they'd never found the body, how she'd known, the second she saw Alex Moorehead's face on the television when he was arrested, that this was the man who had killed her son.

'The women you spoke to earlier,' he said. 'You know there's nothing you can do?'

'Why show me this?'

142

'Look at the others.'

I did.

Shivered when I saw the photos of her with an older gentleman and her son, the three of them walking together along Broughty Ferry Beach, holding ice-cream cones, the son smiling and the old man looking more content than I'd ever known him to be. Back in the days when he had a full head of hair.

'Face it,' Griggs said. 'No matter where you go in this city, you can't escape him.'

'This is a joke,' I said. 'Photoshop, some shite like that? I didn't think you'd take it so far as trying to fuck with my head.'

Griggs smiled. 'They were neighbours, nothing more. The old man probably never made the connection between Alex Moorehead and the young lad's disappearance. He'd have heard third-hand. But when they lived next door to each other, Burns used to take an interest. A neighbourly interest. She was a single mother, after all, and her boy was boisterous. I'm not saying there was anything sexual.'

There wouldn't have been. David Burns took his self-proclaimed role as a family man seriously. He had never betrayed his wife. Not beyond lying to her about how he made his money. And even then, it was a lie in which she willingly participated.

'Why are you showing me this?'

'I'm showing you that you have another

143

way in, McNee. That maybe there are different ways to gain his trust. Sometimes a shared cause can—'

'Why are you so desperate? You've had more than enough opportunities to put people in with Burns before. What makes me so special?'

'Three years ago, you'd have killed yourself to put him away. I've read your file. Probably know you better than you know yourself.'

'Don't give me that shite,' I said.

People told me that constantly, that they knew me, that they understood who I was. Sometimes, I think, they meant it. Looking at myself in a mirror, sometimes I tried to understand what that meant. What they told me they understood was often something I never saw in myself.

Which meant what, precisely? That I was deluding myself? That they were more perceptive than I could ever hope to be?

Or that somehow I was a human mirror? That when people looked at me, they didn't really see the person I was, but whatever they were looking for in the first place: themselves.

As an investigator, you become whatever you need to be to get the job done. You develop personality traits to suit the situation, to get whatever it is you need for someone else. Similar in some ways to being a cop. I joined the force when I was nineteen, became what I thought was the model copper. And then when I quit, moved almost immediately into the investigation business. Why? Because it was the only thing that suited the skills I had, because it allowed me to do the only thing I knew how to do and yet still remove myself from everything that was slowly driving me insane.

Had I lost something of myself because of all that?

Become a reflection for other people's emotions?

Except that Griggs hit it right about a couple of things. A few years ago, even if it had meant harming myself, I would have done anything to take down Burns. He was the Enemy, the one I had chosen to represent everything that was wrong in the world.

And at the same time, he chose me as some twisted reflection of himself.

I'd never understood that. But maybe now I could.

What had changed in me over the years? Why was I now unwilling to sacrifice myself for what I saw as a greater good? It wasn't just about the pretence of working with a scumbag like Burns. No, it was deeper than that.

My life had changed.

I had changed.

I was rebuilding myself. Becoming a whole person. Picking up the pieces years after the accident had shattered me. I had forced myself to become more than simply a mirror for other people's worst emotions. If Griggs persuaded me to go undercover, then it would feel as though I had lost all of the progress I had made. As though I was losing the part of myself that finally felt human.

Griggs was asking me to sacrifice the peace of mind I had finally achieved for the sake of bringing down one man. And no matter what Burns had done, I wasn't sure I could sacrifice all of that any more.

Because if I went back that way again, I don't know if I could come back.

I shook my head. 'Either way, I'm screwed. And if you were so confident that I was the right man for the job, you wouldn't be trying to blackmail me.'

Griggs said, 'It's not blackmail.'

'What is it, then?'

'You need to know we're serious.'

'I can't do it.'

'You said it yourself: you're fucked either way.'

'Aye,' I said. 'There's that.'

'The charges make for the best cover story.'

'I'd serve time. Even when I got out, I couldn't just pick up from where I'd left off.'

'We'd do our best to help—'

I shook my head. 'Do it or don't do it,' I said. 'Don't waste my time or patience.'

'You know what Burns does. What he did to your friend, Ernie Bright.'

'Aye,' I said, 'exactly what you're doing to me.' I stood up, signalling that I wanted him out of my office. 'I used to respect you. Everyone on the force looked up to you. You were one of the good guys. You'd battled your demons, become a decent man. I remember when they tried to hang an excessive force on you, and you beat it because you had the support and respect of everyone around you. Think they'd still feel the same knowing what you were doing here?'

'This is a bigger picture, McNee.'

'Bigger picture my arse,' I said. 'Get out. Tell Kellen to file her charges if it makes you feel better to screw with someone's life. Even if I have to serve time, I'm not doing this. I'm not your guy, Griggs.'

'You'll change your mind,' Griggs said.

I didn't say anything.

He got the hint, finally, and walked out.

I watched out the window, saw him cross the street and walk to the car park at the rear of the Overgate Centre.

When he was out of sight, I grabbed a coffee mug from my desk and flung it against the wall.

Watching it shatter didn't make me feel any better.

NINETEEN

Jonathan Moorehead did not return home.

Four days and counting.

I had seen something in his face when I talked to him. Something that told me I had awoken old ghosts.

The questions that seized him the first time we talked were understandable:

Why me? Was there something I could have done?

Normal questions. The kind any normal person might have if their son had done such monstrous things.

I wonder if he had managed to come to terms with them over the years, or at least forget them. And if my visit opened up those old wounds, made them fresh once more.

The one thing I knew was the one thing he could not listen to.

Monsters do not always beget monsters. The father is not always responsible for the son.

As human beings we make our own way in life. Other people can give us a nudge along the way, but sometimes we are just made to be a certain way and nothing anyone does can push us off that path.

But I was also beginning to suspect that Alex Moorehead was not the man or the monster we had painted him to be.

The man I met all those years ago, and again just a few weeks earlier, was not a cold, vicious, calculating sociopath. He was a man who had retreated into himself. I suspect that if he felt he could have talked about what happened to all those other victims, he would have.

But something was preventing him from doing that. And no one seemed to be able to work out what that something was. For years now, no one had been able to understand what was going on inside his head.

Thinking about it, with a little distance, knowing what I did about what finally happened to him, I was beginning to realize what it might be.

Fear.

Not of being found out. It was too late for that.

No, there had been something else in Alex Moorehead's attitude. Something deeper and more primal than the fear of secrets yet to be uncovered.

I called an old friend who worked in archives, asked her to pull files on Moorehead. 'The ones Ernie submitted.'

'I can't,' she told me over the line. 'They're

sealed and confidential.'

'Alex Moorehead is dead. I was one of the original investigating officers.'

'They're not for release to private citizens.'

'Why?'

She hesitated. 'Normally, I guess I'd consider it a favour ... but given all the shite you've brought down on this department recently...'

'I assisted Ernie on the original investigation. Besides, he's dead. He's not going to care—'

'I'm putting my neck out for you. You understand that?'

'I know,' I said. Feeling a lump in my throat. A hesitancy, knowing what I had to say to her. 'But you've got kids, Aileen. Can you imagine what it would feel like to lose them?'

'Don't you bloody dare...'

'I was asked to look into this by a woman whose child was taken from her. A woman who doesn't know what happened to her child, but who believed that Alex Moorehead had all the answers.'

'You're a bastard, McNee.'

Someday, I'll write a book: *How to Lose Friends and Alienate People*.

But not today.

There are times when you have to pull out dirty tricks, distasteful as that can be. Even when you're dealing with someone you like

150

and respect. But you have to know that the tricks will work. You have to have no other choice. I was walking a fine line with Aileen. The wrong tone, even for a second, and I'd lose her completely.

'Please,' I said. 'No one will know.'

She was quiet on the other end of the line. I had to swallow, tried not to make a noise as I did so.

'I'll see what I can do,' she said. 'But if anyone asks, you and I haven't talked in years.'

'Fair enough,' I said. 'You're doing the right thing.'

She didn't respond to that. All she did was hang up.

The copied files came encrypted, forwarded from a temporary and anonymous email address. Aileen wasn't taking any chances. I couldn't blame her.

As for the consequences if any leaks came back to me, hell, if Griggs was serious with his threats, then it didn't matter what I did any more. Compared to a manslaughter charge – they wouldn't get me on murder; I was confident about that, at least – this was chicken feed.

I transferred the files across to an older machine, disconnected it from the network. Feeling oddly paranoid about the whole affair. Perhaps Griggs really did have me rattled, no matter what I told him or myself.

Maybe he was watching my every move, looking to compound error with error. So, sure, I wanted to give him the middle finger, but I didn't want to look sloppy doing it.

15/09/06

DI ERNIE BRIGHT: Tell me how it felt to kill him. To kill Justin.
ALEX MOOREHEAD: It didn't feel good.
EB: How didn't it feel good? I need specifics, Alex. We need to talk about this. If you talk about this, you'll feel better.
AM: Confession is good for the soul?
EB: I thought we were past this. The tough talk, I mean. The attitude. You've confessed, Alex. What we need to do now is help you to put your side of the story across.
AM: I mean that ... I mean, I didn't mean to...
EB: The wounds were deliberate, Alex. The medical experts confirmed that much. You knew what you were doing to Justin.
AM: No, it was a moment ... a moment ... I didn't think ... it just ... like a switch went off in my brain ... Like...
EB: They said that you could have conceivably killed a boy before. I don't doubt the truth of what they told me, Alex.
AM: No, that's not ... No, it was an accident. I didn't mean to...
EB: Did you fantasize about that, Alex?

About killing a boy? The images we found on your computer, they weren't innocent art. They weren't downloaded by accident. They were the kind of images you would have to look for. Doesn't matter what the *Daily Mail* says, you don't just stumble across images of abuse on the internet. And you certainly don't accidentally download them and hide them on your hard drive.

AM: Oh God ... (sobs)

17/09/06

EB: How are you feeling today, Alex?

AM: Fuck you.

EB: OK, so we had a little falling out last time we talked. Please, Alex, I'm just trying to get a full picture here. Because the story you tell us doesn't entirely match the facts.

AM: Where's my solicitor?

EB: You want your solicitor now? It's a little late. You've already admitted to killing Justin. You're not coming back from that. You can't.

AM: I told you, I...

EB: I know, Alex. I know. You've played the same tune over and over again. But you and I both know the truth. Because you always hit the same bum notes.

AM: No, no...

EB: Is it something you think about? Do you dream about it, Alex? Is that what it is?

AM: (muffled)

EB: Was it something you couldn't control? With Justin, I mean. Like when you can't stop yourself reaching for another glass of wine in the evening?

AM: Don't...

EB: Don't what?

AM: Do that.

EB: Do what? Cheapen what you do? Children aren't like glasses of wine, are they? They're special, every one of them. Unique. Snowflakes. All of those kids in those pictures, there was no one else like them, was there?

AM: Shut up! Shut up! Shut up!

[sounds of a struggle.]

EB: Suspect restrained and detained. Interview terminated at 14.22 hours.

By this point in the investigation, I was on medical leave following the accident that would lead to my leaving the force. DCI Wood had stepped into my role. The last thing on my mind was Alex Moorehead.

I had never looked at the transcripts before.

You could feel Ernie's frustration building with each interview. And Wood never seemed to say a word, even if he was present in the room every time. No wonder Ernie finally palmed the case off on Wemyss. Alex Moorehead didn't want to talk about what he'd done, almost as though he was deliberately misleading himself about the history of the case. It came across as though he was in denial of his own confession. Like he wanted to take it back, but was too afraid to come out and say so.

I had to wonder if this self-deception was what would lead him to deny the other murders. The only other explanation was that his initial confession had been a lie. One that he was regretting but did not know how to back away from.

Newspaper reports would claim in later years that he showed a distinct lack of remorse. Cod-psychologists and true-crime writers would refer to his own 'supreme' delusions or the fact that he seemed to be trying to distance himself from what he'd done.

Nobody harboured any doubt that in some fashion he was responsible for many deaths and disappearances. This, even though Amityville had only ever produced circumstantial evidence at best, which is why it was running now on one lonely cop and a dwindling budget.

All the same, for Alex Moorehead, one admission had opened up a lifetime of possible charges.

Reading the transcripts, I began to wonder if Alex truly believed himself to be innocent despite what he appeared to be saying. Why admit one killing and not the others? Even Peter Tobin, Scotland's most prolific serial murderer, boasted of at least forty-eight murders, while perhaps not admitting to their full details. But Alex Moorehead denied every charge Amityville brought before him, save Justin's murder, while simultaneously failing to provide any explanation for his innocence.

After a couple of hours locked up inside with only transcripts for company, I left the offices, took a walk down the road to the Howff Cemetery. The Cemetery is an old part of the city, built over the site of an abbey that burned down in 1548, and there is a sense when you walk among the old stones that here is a place that will remain untouched by the ever-changing city around it. Dundee is a city that sometimes seems in danger of losing its own identity through a series of 'modernization' initiatives from the sixties onwards, but in the Howff, the world seems calm and still, not resistant to change so much as immune to it.

I sat down on a bench beneath the overhanging branches of an old tree that seemed to cradle the graves around it, protecting them from the world at large.

I thought about what I was doing.

I was looking for answers to support my own theories. Or rather, those of my clients. I wanted to give them the answers they needed, because it would help them to move on. Finding Alex Moorehead innocent – and perhaps someone else guilty – would give some meaning to the years of doubt that they had all suffered. There would be fresh pain, certainly, and even more questions, but some sense of closure would be attained.

Perhaps we might even have answers as to why these children had to die.

But was this a fantasy? Was I as deluded as some people claimed my clients to be?

Why was I so certain I could find something where others had failed?

I had been as convinced as Ernie that Moorehead was the killer. I had also been convinced in later years, that he had killed before. My assumption based on the evidence surrounding the body of Justin Farnham, and the circumstances uncovered by Wemyss and Project Amity, linking him to the other deaths and disappearances.

Moorehead was not a pleasant man. When he finally admitted that he couldn't escape the truth any more, he became arrogant and confrontational. Ernie had called him on his bullshit, but all the same he put on a show for our benefit; his way of not giving up the power he held.

Was I missing something?

I sat there for a long time, underneath the embrace of the overhanging tree, listening to the dampened sounds of the city that came from nearby, the noise of traffic dulled as though in respect for this final resting place in the heart of the city.

I closed my eyes.

Someone sat next to me.

Susan – her hair longer than I remembered, maybe a little darker, too – smiled, not quite meeting my eyes as though embarrassed at us meeting this way again. 'Steed,' she said, 'I think we should talk.'

TWENTY

'When did you get back?'

'A while ago.'

'You didn't call.'

She brushed a strand of hair away from her face. Kept her head slightly bowed, looking at the ground instead of at me. Something in her body language made me think of a guilty teenager. 'I didn't know if you'd want me to.'

An excuse? Something she wasn't telling me?

She was acting like a stranger.

Less than six months ago, we'd been each other's touchstones. Now she was acting like she didn't know what to say to me any more.

'You know I wanted you to call. I sent emails. I waited for you to reply. And you never...'

'I didn't know what to say.'

'So why turn up like this? Why here?' The unasked question: *Why now?* Given everything that was happening, I couldn't take her sudden reappearance as a coincidence.

She finally looked at me, the hint of a smile at the corners of her mouth. Tugging at her features, but unable to break past the awkwardness of our meeting. And whatever it was she wanted to tell me.

'Steed...' she said, but she had no words to follow my old nickname.

'Just tell me,' I said.

'I left the force ... Came back to the country about two months ago. I'm ... I'm working with the SCDEA now.'

She might as well have stabbed me. Slashed my throat. Stuck kitchen scissors through my eyeballs, into my brain.

'You're working with Griggs,' I said.

'What have you done with yourself the last six months?' she asked. 'I've seen the files. You've been taking on cases that you don't really need to think about. Easy money jobs. Quick-fix investigations. Killing time because you don't know what else to do.' Again, there was that hesitation. But this time she allowed herself to speak. 'Because you were always good at finding ways to distract yourself from the bigger, more personal questions...'

'You take a course in psychology while you were gone?'

'No need when we lived together over a year.' The words snapped out hard, the same effect as a whip cracking across my face. 'I'm sorry,' she said, more softly. 'I didn't mean to...'

'No,' I said. 'You did. I can take it.'

'You always wanted to take Burns down,' she said. 'Now's your chance to actually...'

'You said you know me,' I said. 'But you let Griggs crash into my life like a fucking earthquake. I want to take the bastard down, all right, but I'm doing it on my own terms. You know Griggs is manipulating me, right? Asking questions that have already been answered. Painting me in the worst light he can and then coming forward like he's my fucking saviour.' The old anger welled up inside me. Started in the chest, became this tight and unbearable sensation, spread out through my arms, all my muscles tensing, my fingers flexing. 'You want that, too? Want me to give up my life for the greater good? Is that it? Some higher fucking purpose.'

'You know what Burns has done, Steed. The lives he's ruined.'

'How long have you been working for Griggs?' I asked. 'How long did it take to brainwash you?'

'Don't do this.'

'You didn't come here today because you wanted to. You didn't come here because you cared or because you thought I was making some kind of mistake. You came because your boss told you to. And because no matter how long you went away, you still want to take revenge on Burns for what he did to your father.'

'Steed...'

'Jesus Christ, what do they do to people there? I used to respect Griggs. I always respected you. I...' There were words I wanted to say, but they stumbled, faltered. I wondered if my inability to say them had played a part in her leaving. I cleared my throat, took another run up, let the anger guide me. 'And now rather than ask me right out, he bullies me with one of the weakest efforts at emotional blackmail that ... Christ, Susan, I thought you were—'

'You know what I think?' Susan said, as she stood up. 'That you've become so damn good at lying to yourself about things, at closing off your emotions, at making excuses, that you don't even know you're doing it any more. This is our best shot at Burns, Steed. You are our best shot. I know you can do it. I know you want to do it. Sandy's gone about this like a bull in a china shop, but he knew he'd need to work hard to get you onside. You always said you worked best when backed into a corner.' She leaned over and kissed me on the cheek. As she did so, she slipped something into the breast pocket of my jacket. 'Change your mind,' she said. 'You call me. But don't take too long. Sandy's serious. He'll follow through on his promises.'

I had no doubt about that. None at all.

TWENTY-ONE

I can't escape him.

He's been part of my life so long, I can't imagine what it would be like if he was gone.

Arrested. Dead. Whatever.

What happens when David Burns finally gets what's coming to him?

You might call it an obsession. Maybe it is at that. Something passed down to me from Ernie, who had formed his own obsession with Dundee's 'Godfather' following the force's attempts to strike a deal with the old bastard in the mid-nineties. Ernie had been the go-between, something he'd never been happy about. It was an assignment that would colour the rest of his life.

I often wondered if he'd passed the obsession on to me. A kind of legacy.

Those old photographs. Showing Burns in happy little domestic scenes with one of the Disappeared. Walking the beach with a child and his mother. Acting like a genial old man. A friend. A neighbour.

Griggs presenting them to me because he knew I couldn't resist.

Burns had never been part of the original investigation into Alex Moorehead. And even though I knew that Griggs was pointing me towards the big man for his own reasons, there was still the possibility of finding something that we had overlooked.

Burns would want to help.

A child had been murdered. Burns called himself a family man. Took the description seriously.

I wonder if it's part of the criminal mind, a kind of low-level psychopathy. A man like Burns will deal drugs to whoever wants them. He'll hurt mothers' sons, kill men's brothers, order terrible vengeance on those who have wronged. Yet if someone else behaves in ways that reflect his own actions, he takes offence; vows revenge.

And he'll never accept his own complicity in the cycle of violence.

He answered the door himself, dressed in a dark blue shirt and white trousers. Gave me the eye. After all, our last meeting had hardly been cordial.

'You here because of that prick Griggs?'

'You know I won't work for him.'

Burns nodded. 'One thing I can always count on, your sense of morality. Always thinking you're doing the right thing.'

'I want to talk about Moorehead. Your connection to him.'

He took a slow breath, and said, 'You're

too late, pal. Should have asked me after you arrested him. Not that I knew then. Took a couple of years, aye? Before the truth came out in full.' He looked around, as though he thought we were being watched. 'You like to walk?' When I didn't say anything, he expanded on the question: 'The countryside. Fresh air. Where no one else can hear what you're saying.'

'Aye,' I said. 'I like to walk.'

We took his car across the water, to Norman's Law on the other side of the Tay. Much of the hill is used as farmland, but ramblers and walkers use the more public areas of the hill on a regular basis.

We trudged along a relatively light slope, through ankle-high grass still wet from the rain. I wasn't wearing the right kind of shoes for the walk, and could feel the damp soak through into my socks. I curled my toes inside my shoes with every step. As we neared the edge of fields and enclosures, Highland cows and sheep ambled forward to examine us curiously, maybe sensing that we weren't the usual recreational ramblers.

When we were far enough along, Burns said, 'I hear he killed himself.'

'You knew one of the children he killed.'

'The cunt.'

'The mother lived close to you. You knew the family.'

'That boy should never have died.'

'Why didn't you do anything?'

'At the time, we didn't know that...'

'I mean later. When he was sent to prison. When it came out about the other children. When that lad's name was released. You had the power to do something. And don't you dare deny it.'

Of course he had the power. Back when one of the thugs who had tried to kill me in the graveyard survived and was sent to prison, he was murdered by another inmate. Everyone knew that had been Burns's influence. Everyone knew how far the old man's reach extended.

Burns didn't say anything for a moment. He stopped walking, turned to face me. 'He should have died. He should have been fucking murdered. Not a quick death; he deserved to fucking suffer for what he did to those boys. Animals like him ... No sympathy. You don't give them sympathy. They never show their victims any.'

'So why didn't he? Suffer, I mean.'

Burns hesitated.

'Don't play coy,' I said. 'We both know what you're capable of.'

Burns stepped forward. I held out my hands, posed like Jesus on the cross, let him pat me down. When he was happy, he stepped back. I saw tears in his eyes, but it could have just been the wind. 'Who says I didn't

166

try? And that the hit was fucked. After that, security around the bastard got tight. Soon enough I had bigger problems. There are always bigger problems. You don't deal with something right away, something else always comes up. I should have fucking done it, though. Sooner rather than later.'

'What went wrong?'

'The boy I sent in got the wrong pervert. Can you believe it? After that Moorehead was put in solitary himself. For his own protection. Like he was the victim. Bloody fuck!' He shook his head. Expression on his face said he didn't know whether to laugh or cry. 'I got him a cushy fucking job in the kitchen. Supposed to put glass, you know, in the arsewipe's dinner. Ground glass. You eat a plateful of ground glass and it churns up your insides. Nothing anyone can do for you. Not if they don't know what's happening. So this particular con who owes me a favour, he does this favour, and he gets the wrong bloody pervert's plate. Puts the glass in the wrong food. Jesus, you should have seen the shitstorm after that one.'

I didn't know about the failed hit. Never heard anything from anyone about some prisoner putting glass in the solitary meals. Wondered if it happened while I was in hospital. Or while I was busy feeling sorry for myself, practising my self-destructive tendencies.

The wind picked up a little. It tickled around my exposed skin. Cold and unsettling.

'Think he's guilty, then?'

'No doubt in my mind, son.'

'Why?'

'What the fuck're you so interested for?'

'There's been doubt raised.'

'Then why would the wee prick admit to—?'

'To that one crime and not the rest?'

'He was a psycho! They don't need a bloody reason, lad. Surely you've seen enough in your time to know that.'

I thought of a big, bearded man proudly boasting about the way he'd battered a woman, eventually bashing her brains out in the rear kitchen of an abandoned croft. A man to whom violence came as instinctually as breathing. The very definition of a psychopath. His name was Wickes and I had trusted him up to a point. Two years ago, and I still had nightmares about the violence he had brought into my life.

'Moorehead was different,' I said. 'I've met psychopaths and sociopaths before. Seen them at their worst. Moorehead was ... just ... Did you ever actually talk to him?'

'No. Why would I want to breathe the same air as that pervert?'

'I don't think I noticed it at the time. I was too green. In awe of Ernie, I guess.' I hesitated. 'But when I spoke to him the other week, there was ... when he spoke ... I don't...'

'You think he's innocent?'

Did I nod? Shrug? I don't know. It was hard to put my feelings on the matter into words. Alex Moorehead was accused of a horrendous crime, and like Burns, I believed a man guilty of those crimes should suffer. But if there was even the slightest chance that Alex Moorehead was innocent, then he couldn't simply be punished to make us all feel better, to satiate our desire for revenge. If he was innocent, he'd been harmed as much as the victims of whoever had killed these children.

'You're like a dog with a bone, son,' Burns said. 'Most men would just accept what they were told. But you ... you're different.'

I wondered if this was a compliment. Or something else.

'But I have to ask who it was led you to me. I have my suspicions. But then maybe I'm just a paranoid old fuck. Tell you what, you go find whatever it is you're looking for. Because I can't help you. But I want to know. Come back. Show me your truth, I'll show you mine.' He smiled, then, and I noticed his incisors, the way they stood out, sharp like a wolf's. 'I think you'll find mine very interesting.'

I didn't know what to say. Settled for

silence on the matter.

He was goading me with something. I didn't know what.

'Come on, then,' he said, looking up at the sky. 'It's getting chilly, eh? An old man can only take so much fresh air.'

TWENTY-TWO

I was at a dead end. No way forward.

All Burns had told me was that, like everyone else, once the monster was caged, he'd moved on with his life.

Anger and outrage only lasts so long. For most people.

I thought about Susan, about what she'd said earlier. Deliberately trying to provoke me into action, but for her own reasons.

Had she changed so much?

Could I blame her if she had?

The question of Ernie Bright's guilt or innocence was thorny at best. But I did know that he had some kind of special relationship with Burns. Not quite friendship, but something else.

Utilitarian perhaps. Aristotelian.

I used to know a guy studied philosophy at university. Switched halfway through and became a solicitor, so maybe the ethics course didn't take. He talked about how Aristotle defined friendship at different levels. Utilitarian friends hung out because it was to their mutual advantage. Perhaps, in his own way, Ernie had been trying to use

Burns. He'd certainly tried to do so under the orders of his superiors back in the mid-nineties. Maybe he'd found something in the relationship that continued to be useful even when the operation had ended.

Or perhaps there had been something darker at work.

Not corruption. Ernie had been posthumously cleared of any charges of out-and-out corruption. But there were still lingering questions even a year after his death.

Without Ernie alive to talk, or Burns himself willing to say anything, no one would ever know the full truth. That had to be eating at Susan. She had almost killed a man to clear her father's name, and now she would never really know the truth. She had to deal every day with the knowledge of who had killed her father. Not the trigger man, but the man who had screwed up Ernie Bright's life so completely. She knew that Burns was walking around scot-free, and she couldn't do anything about it.

Susan was a cop from a family of cops. Her father, her grandfather, had been on the force. It was all she knew, part of who she was. Which meant that anything she did had to be within the system. Unlike me, she couldn't walk away from the world of rules and regulations. She heard the voice of her father, and even if he had not been the man she thought she knew, her memories were of the good copper, the man who insisted on everything being done within the restrictions of the law.

When she had come to me at the Howff, she was not looking for a friend or seeking to help me. She knew who I had been, and she wanted to satiate her desire for revenge through me. I could do the things she couldn't bring herself to do.

I was no longer a friend. I was a tool; something she could use.

That was why she'd backed Griggs's play to try and get me close to Burns.

Family.

Family.

Where was Jonathan Moorehead? What did he say to his son?

Back at the office, I dived back into the documents and transcripts. Went over and over the same words, phrases, looking for something I'd missed earlier. I didn't know what it was, but it had to be there. Just one word out of place. Something that hadn't seemed significant before.

Anything that could help.

Burns had been of no use to me. Just another dead end. A distraction. Part of Griggs's scheme to try and bring us closer. Interviewing him at the time would have done no good. He had merely been the woman's neighbour. He trusted that Ernie and I had done the right thing in arresting Alex.

For once, he had nothing to hide.

Which meant I needed to find something else. Anything. Or was I simply wasting everyone's time looking for shadows?

Two hours later, my vision going fuzzy, I re-read one of the early interviews. A few lines. They hadn't seemed significant before, and yet now seemed somehow important; out of place in a long stream of nothing.

20/10/06

EB: Why did you do it?

AM: Does it matter?

EB: I think it does. Justin's mother thinks it does.

AM: I told you I did it. Why do you keep—?

EB: Call me a curious bastard. You know we found the images?

AM: The images?

EB: Your private collection? (to recorder) I am now showing the suspect printouts of images found on a partitioned drive.

AM: Where did you find—?

EB: They were on your computer, hidden in a partitioned drive. Protected, of course. But we had some help finding them.

AM: Help?

EB: One of your fellow IT geeks. You know Jason Taylor, right?

AM (agitated): Fuck you. Fuck you. Fuck
you.

Jason Taylor

I remembered Jason.

The final piece of the puzzle. The one who
helped seal the case against Alex Moorehead. Ernie had already organized a forensic
team to examine Moorehead's computer.
But they had encountered difficulties with
his security. Typical IT geek, Alex Moorehead's set-up was far from typical. His security was a custom program that none of the
team had ever encountered.

Hence: Jason Taylor.

He had worked alongside Alex before. Had
concerns about his friend's behaviour. He
had stepped forward to ask if he could assist
with decoding Alex's systems, claimed to
know Alex's methodology. They used the
same security measures; unique programs
and algorithms that the two of them had
developed in tandem during their days at
university.

He came recommended, too.

By DCI Wood.

Make of that what you will.

It was Jason who found the images. He had
been the outside contractor who performed
the second sweep of Moorehead's equipment.

The one who vomited when he realized

175

what he had come across. Who nearly broke down in court testifying against his former friend.

Back then, he had been the keystone in the case for the prosecution.

Now I was wondering if perhaps he knew more than he had let on.

Used to be that if all you had to go on was a name, you'd reach a dead end fast. Now all you need is a name, an address (even an old one) and a possible occupation. Sometimes even just the name is more than enough to track down your average citizen in the digital age. None of us really realize how much information there is out there for anyone with the barest minimum of skill to find.

Jason Taylor was running his own web-design company these days. After a few years running anti-virus and security software, he'd clearly decided that the money was in website design.

Redboot.

That's what they called themselves. I didn't know if that was a private joke or some reference I was too out of the loop to understand.

I clicked through to the staff page, then again through to Taylor's biography. His picture was stark black and white, showed a handsome-looking man with big eyes and long dark hair. He was in his mid-forties, had an intense aura about him. You imagined he never wanted to leave the office, that if he had a wife and children then he was an invisible presence in their lives.

But the biography didn't say anything about family. Taylor was all business:

Jason Taylor founded Redboot over five years ago from the garage of a friend's house with little more than a laptop computer and a desire to deliver the best possible website design for a select list of local clients. Since then, Redboot has expanded under Jason's leadership to become a national leader in web design and marketing.

No real personal detail. No heart-warming throwaways about living in the country with a wife, a dog and the obligatory 2.4. The man with the expensive haircut and the intense stare either had nothing to say or nothing he wanted to say.

There was some value in that. Some people like to keep their personal and professional lives separate. Who needs to know about your domestic situation when they're hiring you to promote their brand.

There was a contact number for the company as well as online support forms and some generic company email addresses. I didn't use them, though. I was just doing recon work, trying to figure if my gut instinct was correct or if I had finally allowed my own paranoia to dictate my actions.

TWENTY-THREE

I looked back through the files that Aileen had sent me. Jason Taylor was little more than a footnote. The information was scant. At the time we interviewed him, Taylor had been working on security software he intended for commercial release. He told us it was based on something he'd worked with Alex Moorehead on before Alex decided to go freelance, work on other people's problems.

Taylor and Alex Moorehead had shared residences at university together for two years before moving out. They then shared a flat, started work on the anti-virus software and set up their own limited company which Moorehead left six months later. There was no real reason given other than he wasn't fully dedicated to the idea, worried about being his own boss.

I remembered Taylor as cocky; absolutely certain of himself in the way that only the privileged can be. He had been privately educated, had that edge of arrogance that sometimes comes through instead of the in-

178

tended confidence. Not great for getting on with everyone, but fantastic for steamrollering through life. When he'd talked to us, I always had the feeling it was with barely disguised contempt, as though he figured we were a little slow.

Moorehead used the systems that he and Taylor had developed on his own PC. At the time Taylor claimed the anti-intruder measures made Norton and the market-leaders look like kid-on safes, the kind of plastic shite a kid might keep his wee pennies in.

Did I want to talk to him again? In case we missed something? In case he missed something?

It was nearly six years later. I'd already fucked up by talking to the father. Was I dragging up the past for no reason?

I killed time by re-reading some of the papers that the ABI had sent me along with the letter detailing my suspension from the organization. A knot built up inside me, and a feeling of nausea made me swallow repeatedly.

I thought about Kellen.

She was after me. Convinced of my guilt. She didn't know me. Had no personal stake in anything I had ever done to the department. And yet she was still certain I was culpable in terms of the charges being made against me.

In the back of my mind, the question

lurked: what if she was right?

I had killed a man. Lied to the authorities about the exact nature of his death. I had covered up the truth.

Sooner or later I'd have to pay.

Kellen wasn't going to give up. All I could do was sit tight and see what happened.

Maybe Griggs's offer was the best option I had. Susan was right, after all: taking down Burns would fulfil a long-held ambition. Of mine. Of her father's.

But in the meantime, I looked like a criminal myself.

Without the job, who was I? How did I define myself?

I checked the clock. It was getting late in the afternoon. I couldn't just sit around and feel sorry for myself.

So I dialled through to Redboot.

The receptionist asked me for my name. I gave it as 'Detective Constable McNee. He might not remember me. Tell him it's to do with his old friend Alex.'

When he came on the line, he sounded hesitant. 'It's been a long time. You could have dropped me an email.'

'It's easy to ignore an email.'

'What's this about?'

'Alex Moorehead. You know he killed himself?'

'Christ!' There was a flatness to his voice.

'Mr Taylor, in the interest of disclosure I

should point out I am no longer a police officer. I'm a private citizen now. I work as a private investigator. I was asked to examine new evidence in the Moorehead case before he died.'

'He was my friend,' Taylor said. 'He was my friend and he betrayed not only me, but everyone who knew him. In the worst possible fashion. I did my public service helping to put a monster like that away.' The formality in his tone hid any upset that might have been trying to break through. He might have been a bad actor reading from a script.

'I know what you did, Mr Taylor,' I said. 'I'm merely trying to see if there's anything we missed in the initial investigation.'

'Why?'

Should I tell him the truth? Would it be what he wanted to hear? What he needed to hear? How much did I tell this man? How much did he know? How much was he hiding?

I've learned over the years that whether we mean to or not, we all hide things. We all have secrets. Some secrets could change our world entirely. Others were mere red herrings, things that could terrify us when kept in the deep dark corners of our mind where we preferred to hide them, but that when exposed to the harsh light of the world became merely mild embarrassments or odd non-entities that we would later struggle to explain why they held such power over us.

Which kind of secret did a man like Taylor hold?

'I'm working for a private client,' I said, omitting the detail that I was working for several individuals. Keeping it simple, keeping it anonymous. What good would it do to even hint that I was working for the mothers of the disappeared? 'One who has a personal interest in Mr Moorehead's case. In particular, his motivations.'

'His motivations? Christ, man, he was a monster! A fucked-up aberration of the human species. I know some people like to try and humanize monsters like Alex, but there's no use hiding the truth.' There was an edge to his voice that sounded almost manic, a far cry from the controlled and eloquent tones of just a few minutes earlier.

'So there was nothing you can think of that might have caused him to—'

'If I had seen anything like that,' Taylor said, 'I'd have told someone. What he did was sickening. More than sickening. He had pictures of kids – bloody kids – on his computer. He killed little boys. He ... he...'

'He what?'

'I don't know. He did things to them. I don't even want to...'

I had lost him. I knew that. We had only a few seconds left before he hung up the phone and considered the matter closed. I might have considered this to be a bad thing; a lead lost or a fuck-up to be analysed and regretted later. But it was neither of those things. What it was, was a way forward, an indication that I was on the right path.

In the initial interviews, when Ernie mentioned Taylor's name to Moorehead, he'd shouted at Ernie to fuck himself, started his descent into near-complete silence about the nature of his crimes.

At the time, Ernie had assumed that Moorehead finally realized the magnitude of what he'd done.

Reading the transcript with the benefit of years of distance, I read a fear between the lines that made me wonder if it wasn't the idea of what he'd done that scared him, but the name that Ernie threw at him.

They had been what you might call best friends. They should have known each other's secrets.

And now, Jason Taylor's reaction told me something new. He knew more than he'd ever admitted to anyone. He knew things that would shed light on the truth behind the monster known as Alex Moorehead. He just had to tell someone about them. Get over the fear he'd been living with for the past six years, bring the truth out into the light.

TWENTY-FOUR

That night, I slept in fits and starts. I don't remember good dreams. Only the bad ones ever stay with me; the dreams that threaten to kill you in your sleep, grabbing hold of the deepest, darkest places in your mind and refusing to let go until they've pulled out everything that's in there.

I was standing in the centre of the anonymous incident room that Wemyss had set up at Kirkcaldy FHQ. Alone, looking at the images on the walls and finding myself flinching every time I saw one of the boys staring out at me. There was something wrong with the images. They were no longer smiling, carefree snaps of lives lost before they had a chance to be lived. Instead, each of the boys stared out of the confines of their photographs with an unnatural and terrifying intensity. As though they were looking at the very person who had taken away their lives.

I wanted to say, 'It wasn't me. There was nothing I could have done,' but they continued to stare, and I knew that they didn't care for my excuses.

184

I should have avenged them. But I failed.

There was a cold wind. I shivered, realized that someone had left the door open. I could walk out. But I was stuck where I was, unable to move. Because I was waiting for someone. I didn't know who. But they were coming, I could sense it.

I didn't want them to come. I knew that when they arrived, they would bring the horror of death.

I could have run. Should have run. The door was open. All it took was a moment's decision and I could have avoided facing what I already knew was coming.

But I couldn't move. I just stood where I was, the eyes of the dead on me, blaming me, screaming silently for something I couldn't understand.

And then I became aware of whatever it was finally approaching, turning so that I faced that open door and looked out into the grey corridor beyond. The corridor was unnaturally long and empty. I sensed the visitor walking towards the door from outside, even if I couldn't see them.

The figure was indistinct at first, more a cloud of smoke than a person. It gathered weight as it advanced towards the door, features slowly coming into focus. It looked human.

But I did not want to see the truth of whatever it was.

All I wanted to do was run.

Just as it came into focus, I woke up. Fumbling, I rolled over in bed and reached for the lamp, as though it would somehow dispel whatever lurked in the shadows of my bedroom. It was a childlike terror, and one that my adult brain would mock when it came fully awake, but one that felt urgent and so utterly real that I would do anything to dispel it.

I lay there, awake, the bedside light harsh, yet oddly comforting. After a while the dream faded and I turned off the light. When I finally drifted off, I found myself back in the room.

Waiting.

The third time this happened, I couldn't wake up. I was aware of being stuck in a dream, and somehow this made the process of waking even more difficult. As though by knowing that I could escape, somehow the very act became impossible. The smoke-like figure took on detail and form before my eyes. I couldn't move or even make a sound to try and shock myself back to the land of the living.

Paralysed.

I realized, as the figure came into focus, that there was one picture missing from the wall. One boy whose face had not glared at me with a kind of pitying hatred. He was the one I feared the most, whose retribution and need for revenge was the greatest.

Justin Farnham.

I couldn't look away. His eyes were filled with a violent hatred and desire for revenge. He stood perfectly still, not saying a word.

Slowly, his skin rippled as though made of thin material, with a wind rustling underneath. Marks appeared on his skin; violent red slashes around his face. His eyes roadmapped red before haemorrhaging blood. All the while he remained perfectly still.

Finally, I was able to ask: 'Who did this?'

'You already know.'

His lips didn't move. It was more like a memory of something he might have said. A child's voice that creaked like tombstones rubbing together.

The marks appeared on his neck, his throat opening wide, the blood dark and vibrant as it slid over his pale skin.

I felt sick. My stomach twisted violently.

I woke up then, and was on my feet before I even had a chance to think. Running to the bathroom. As I vomited into the bowl, I felt the bile burn inside my throat. I thought I might choke, that the vomiting might never stop. When it finally did, I spat out what had caught in my teeth and then fell back, lying on the cool of the lino floor, looking up at the lights on the ceiling.

I couldn't close my eyes. Every time I did,

I saw Justin standing before me, his throat slit, his eyes burning at the injustice of his early death.

You already know.

TWENTY-FIVE

'You ever talk to Jason Taylor?'

Wemyss was keeping his distance from me. The tension in his shoulders spoke of his desire to deck me one, but then I figured he'd have to join a long line.

'Once,' Wemyss said. 'That was the friend, right? The one who helped you hack Moorehead's machine?'

'That's him.'

'He didn't have much to say.'

'Yeah?'

'Beyond what he already told Bright, I mean.'

'Bright and Woo—'

'Oh, aye, bring that tube's name up, why don't you? He's Tayside's embarrassment, all right? And we'd prefer it all stayed that way.'

We were talking in the lobby of Kirkcaldy FHQ. He was speaking to me on sufferance only. Mostly because I'd threatened to hang around until he came downstairs. So here we were. Maybe he figured I'd behave myself if we were in public.

Or maybe it was so he'd behave himself. It

189

would be easy to think of Wemyss as fat, but I had the feeling his size was as much muscle as it was bacon rolls.

'So you asked Taylor the same questions as Bright?'

'Anything else I should have asked?'

I didn't say anything.

Wemyss sighed. His shoulders slumped. 'Fucksakes, McNee. Come out and say it, why don't you? We all know that Wood brought Taylor in. Think I didn't start asking myself a few questions last year? I mean, if he was dirty anyway, he might as well be guilty of a million other sins.' Wemyss massaged his forehead with sweaty fingers, like jointed bratwurst. 'You really are a pain in the arse. I mean, everyone warned me, but I figured you had to have something. Truth is, I don't know if you're deluded or if you're stringing along these women for all their worth, giving them hope where you and I both know that there's none.'

'All this is because the charges against me were made public,' I said. 'Before then you had no worries trusting my gut instinct.'

'I had no worries granting you a little professional courtesy,' he said. 'There's a big fuck-off difference, pal.'

'I talked to Taylor earlier,' I said.

'And he told you to piss off?'

'Not in so many words.'

'Pity.'

'Look, I think there's something worth examining here.'

'You're pissing on his grave, you know that? DI Bright, I mean. You already called his name into question ... What, you're not going to rest until you've dragged all the bloody polis through the dirt?'

'I'm the one who cleared him,' I said. 'When everyone else just assumed he was one more corrupt cop.'

'Aye, you cleared him. And implicated one of the finest political movers Tayside Police ever had...'

'I didn't set out after Wood,' I said. 'He put himself in the firing line.'

'You embarrassed Tayside, you know that? The whole force is still having to tiptoe around because of what you did, and now here you are calling your old friend's investigation methods into question?'

'I think he missed something. I think we both did. Hell, I think Wood did. Look, Wood was a drug-dealing, lying bawbag, but I think even he understood what it meant to catch a child-killer. I don't think it was sloppy work. I think—'

'You think you can fix everything. Right? OK, I get it now. You're deluded, McNee. Fucking hero complex. You're fixating on Taylor because you know that you missed something and he's the only lead you have left. You want to give these poor women what

they're looking for. Fine. But you're obses-
sing over the point. You want to let them
know that there are bogey-men out there,
and that there is someone they can hate for
what happened. And you'll do anything to
achieve that.'

I didn't say anything. Maybe because I was
afraid he had a point.

'Just tell them you're off the case, McNee,'
Wemyss said. 'Quit acting the hero. Quit
looking for conspiracies. And go look after
your own fucking house.'

What made me fixate on Taylor?

Taylor had come forward because he wanted to be a responsible citizen. Because he
wasn't as friendly with Alex as we thought.
Or just because hacking into his friend's
computer gave him a challenge.

Nothing there that would raise alarm bells.
Nothing to say that Taylor wasn't just a concerned citizen who recognized something in
his friend that he had never seen before. The
fact that a corrupt bastard like Wood had
vouched for him didn't tell me anything one
way or the other. The official statements
claimed that Taylor had done some freelance
IT work for Wood in the past. Or, to put it
another way, he'd helped fix Wood's computer, once.

But thinking about Taylor, I began to realize how Ernie must have felt about Alex

Moorehead. When he found Justin's body too quickly, too eagerly. The same way that Taylor discovered was just a little too eager to uncover that damning evidence against his friend.

I didn't like it. And maybe I was looking too hard for answers. Wemyss had already bought into the idea that Moorehead may have been innocent, but he was searching for the simplest explanation as to what really happened. Looking at what he knew and deciding that everything pointed towards dear old Dad being the guilty party. An assumption compounded by the old man's sudden disappearance.

Maybe he was right.

Maybe I was overcomplicating the issue.

The last few years had seen more intensity than I cared to remember. Top it off with Griggs handing DS Kellen her investigation on a plate, and I was close to burnout.

Close to crazy?

That evening, I sent a message around the Mothers of the Disappeared. A simple email with an attachment, asking if any of them remembered a friend of Alex's who might have stayed with him. I sent them a picture of Taylor. But as he was now. I had been unable to discover any images of the man he would have been at each disappearance.

I made a late dinner, a quick and easy carbonara that I still managed to spoil by overheating the eggs. I wound up with something that resembled scrambled eggs wrapped around spaghetti more than any light Italian dish.

Just as I was finishing there was a knock at the door. Loud and heavy. Copper's knock. I found Lindsay standing there in the hall. Still using crutches. 'You're not the kind of cunt that would keep an invalid standing on his doorstep, are you?'

And no, I wasn't. But for just a moment, I thought maybe I could be.

TWENTY-SIX

I had some beers in the fridge. Nothing exciting, but enough to appease casual guests. We drank straight from the bottles, Lindsay grabbing the sofa, me taking the armchair by the window.

For a while, neither of us said anything, and then: 'Coppers talk. You know that, right?'

'Sure,' I said.

He nodded, as though digesting what I'd said. Maybe trying to decide if he honestly believed a word that came out of my mouth. For all that had changed between us, there was still an air of distrust that neither of us would ever be able to fully ignore. Call it habit if you like, but it would always be there.

Lindsay had decided he hated me from the moment we met. I'd been much the same. Our mutual loathing had lasted for years.

So how to explain the last few months?

Were we friends now?

Perhaps some shared experiences can transcend the pettiness of what the pop-psychologically inclined call 'personality clash'. Lindsay and I would never be the best of friends, but perhaps we understood each other now in ways we never could before.

'I got a call from Wemyss, over at Kirkcaldy. Telling me how you were up to your old tricks. Of course, it means I'm in the shitter. Because I vouched for you.'

'You think I could let something like this alone?'

'Like what?'

'Like the chance to make sure the right guy paid for what happened to those children.'

He was silent.

'What if it was your boy?'

More silence. Stubborn. How could he ever admit I was right?

'I'd want the cocksucker castrated,' said Lindsay. 'But Alex Moorehead went down for this crime...' Outside of his home, away from his family, he had reverted to the Lindsay I knew and loathed. Foul mouth, snap judgements, little patience. Put me on an even keel, at least.

'You'd have been happy with the lie?'

'If I believed it was the truth. Which I still do. You know I assisted Ernie after your little accident? Took up the slack, so to speak.'

'He never mentioned it,'

'Why would he? Given everything else, how would you feel if you knew I'd come along and nicked the case that was supposed

196

to set you up for a long life at CID?'

I slugged back a mouthful of beer.

Wished I had something stronger.

'You know that Elizabeth Farnham had a little thing for geek boy?'

I shook my head.

'They slept together, her and Alex Moorehead. Three weeks before Justin vanished. She was always calling up Ernie, protesting the prick's innocence. Once we got it out of her, I mean. I always thought, who'd want to admit they slept with a monster? In her mind there had to be a mistake.'

'There was. Even Wemyss admits that.'

'No,' said Lindsay. 'He admits the possibility. There's a big fucking difference. That fat fuck may look like the only two things on his mind are when to eat and when to shite, but he's sharp as a pointy stick up the arse. And he admits you might have a point, despite the fact that you're a shitey wee arsebucket. But that doesn't mean you're right. Just means you might not be wrong. Besides, you're pointing fingers at the wrong people.'

'Really?'

'I used Taylor myself. After that bang-up job he did on Moorehead's system. And, aye, Wood's reference helped. So don't go thinking what I know you're thinking. This was back when IT was small, underfunded, maybe even misunderstood. Although I hesitate to tell the geeks that, you know? I gave the arrogant twat a few calls when we were stuck. He was good, McNee. I mean bona-fide digital dick genius. Wood even offered him a full-time position when Tayside finally started properly building its IT operations and digital forensics.'

'But he turned it down?'

'Better money to be made in the private leisure sector. So he said.'

'Or maybe he was worried you'd get too close to something.'

'Tell me something, McNee. I know I'm a cynical bawbag, but you take the bastard biscuit. You really do. Taylor's probably off the end of the autism scale, but that doesn't make him a criminal genius. Sometimes just because something looks suspicious, doesn't mean it is.'

I nodded.

But I didn't agree with him.

Something about Jason Taylor was rotten, and had been from the moment he offered his services to help bang up his friend.

And I was going to prove it.

TWENTY-SEVEN

Sometimes, even when all the evidence tells you it's a bad idea, you need to follow your instinct.

Wemyss was right that the most likely suspect was the missing father. But there wasn't much more I could do about that than the police were already doing. Besides, what harm could there be in just talking to Taylor? Assuring myself that I was wrong? That he really didn't know anything?

The internet is a wonderful thing. But it's easy to hide behind the anonymity of an email or the relative safety of a phone connection.

Face to face communication gives away a lot. If you want to lie, the worst thing you can do is talk directly to someone. That's one of the reasons police interrogations work best up close and personal. A good copper is not always a trained psychologist – although people are coming to the force through a variety of paths these days – but they quickly develop a good eye for the things that people aren't saying with words. They learn to instinctively read between gestures. They get at the truth and chip away at a person until finally they can no longer hide those things they've been saying all along.

It's about facial tics. Small gestures. Imperceptible eye movements.

The things you see, but don't see.

Intuition is another word for the unconscious. Your mind will pick up on things you can't always consciously articulate.

Crimes committed in the last twenty years will often have an electronic trail. Incriminating emails, phone calls, text messages or a thousand other ways of implicating yourself that you'd never think of in the day-to-day running of things. There is always something visible to the breed of detectives that followed in the lead of willing geeks like Jason Taylor. Information is the new DNA, and if most minor criminal acts are caught by hair fibres or fingerprints, then many other crimes can now be caught by discarded strands of information that even your smarter-than-average crook won't believe to be important.

But confession still comes down to confrontation.

You can follow the evidence all you like, but it's meaningless if you don't understand people. It's the old difference between the letter and spirit of the law. You can arrest someone for breaking the law, but doing so doesn't mean a damn if you don't understand why they did what they did.

It was a two-and-a-half-hour drive to the offices of Redboot, on the upper floor of an unassuming building on the outskirts of Ayr. Not the most salubrious of addresses, but then London, Glasgow and Edinburgh were no longer the centre of the world, and a start-up had as much a chance succeeding out here as anywhere else.

Although if I could have afforded to set up anywhere other than Ayr, I would have given it a go. It's an odd little town. Despite the closeness of the sea, there's an air of better days having been seen and that all-too-familiar feel of the little Scottish town that no longer knows what it is in the grand scheme of things. Birthplace of Burns? Aye, but is that enough to provide a sense of purpose in an age of austerity and recession?

I parked across the street and settled in to wait.

I tilted the seat back, kept the radio on. Flicked through local stations. What I got were DJs trying too hard, and pop songs that came from artists I could no longer readily identify mixed in with embarrassing guff from the eighties and nineties.

Finally I gave up, plugged in the MP3 player, let Nick Cave, Leonard Cohen and ol' Bob Dylan wash over me.

Bob was Tangled Up In Blue when Taylor

left the Redboot offices. He was taller than I expected, walked with a strange, loping gait. It didn't fit with the voice I'd heard on the telephone or the image projected by his picture on the website, but I was beginning to remember him better now. He was a geek trying to hide himself. Someone for whom his natural social awkwardness was a constant embarrassment. Something to be hidden behind carefully considered affectations. This was a man who didn't let you see what he really was.

I got out of the car, rushed to catch him up. He was about to climb into a silver Merc when I called his name.

He turned round, leaned against the car as I walked over to him. 'I could put out an injunction against you,' he said. 'This is harassment.'

I shrugged. 'Persistence.'

'Poh-taye-toh,' he said, 'poh-tah-toh.'

I said, 'Let's call the whole thing off?'

'Yes,' he said. 'Let's.' He still felt he was in control of the situation. His voice retained that strangled attempt at education that covered up his natural accent. I remembered thinking when we first met that he was somehow ashamed of his roots, that everything about him was an affectation. Not that it struck me as a definite problem. He wasn't the first guy to try and leave working-class roots behind.

'You never talked to Alex Moorehead after he was arrested,' I said. 'But before the incident, you were close friends. At least that's the way you spun it.'

He had the car door open. He stood up straight and let go of the handle. 'Would you talk to him? After that?'

'Right.' I waited a moment. 'Because you felt he had betrayed you? Or because you felt you betrayed him?'

'I was hoping I'd find something to exonerate the poor bastard.'

'Looking back on it, I just thought maybe you were a bit quick to lend a hand.'

'Buyer's remorse?'

'Copper's remorse, maybe.'

'Is this why you're no longer on the force? Are you going around, now, trying to screw up all the cases your boss ever made?'

I shrugged.

'Tell me how you define friendship, Mr McNee. I thought we were friends, me and Alex. Then I realized I never knew him. Kind of hard to imagine he was keeping that kind of secret.'

'I've seen people who were betrayed before,' I said. 'Most of them want answers. They feel it so personally, so deep inside them, like a blade stuck between the ribs, that the only way to rid themselves of the echo of that pain is to confront the person who betrayed them and ask one very simple question.'

'Yes.' He regarded me for a moment. Moved his head from one side to the other. Quick and jerky. He held his hands down his sides, arms absolutely still, back ramrod straight, but his fingers twitched incessantly as though they wanted to wrap themselves around something and squeeze.

Maybe my neck. Or the neck of the man he claimed to have betrayed him.

He was tough to read that way.

He said, 'Why? That's the question. You want to ask him, why?'

'But you never did. At least you never asked us. Or him. You came, did what you needed to do, and then you just walked away.'

'I needed to process what I found. I'm sure you dealt with that kind of thing all the time when you were a copper. Me, I'd never seen anything like it before.'

I remembered his reaction. He'd asked to be excused, to take some air, said he'd found something but couldn't put into words what we would see on the screen.

It had seemed genuine enough at the time. Enough that no one had questioned it. Not Ernie. Not Wood.

Was I now rewriting history to fit my current theories?

'Do you mind if I ask ... ?'

He took a deep breath, loud enough to

stop me mid-question. His tongue darted from between his thin lips and dabbed around for a second. Making me think of a lizard who sensed a nearby fly.

'Will it make you leave me alone?'

'If I'm happy with the answer.'

'You're not the police any more,' he said. 'But I could call them, the real police, have them sling your arse inside for harassing a private citizen.'

'Aye, you could,' I said. 'And I'd understand. But all I want is a moment of your time. I need to understand Alex. I need to reassure my clients that the right man paid for his crime. That I didn't overlook anything. To do that I need all the facts at my disposal.'

'And you think talking to me will help?' Was that a slight twitch in his left eye? An involuntary flinch?

'It can't hurt,' I said. 'You knew him, I think, better than anyone.' What I did then was play the deception card. 'The last person he talked to was his father. It was only after that he killed himself. Now his father's disappeared. Coincidence?'

Taylor shrugged.

'I just need a better picture of who Alex was. His relationship to his family, especially. It might help explain some things.'

'I'm not sure I can—'

'Like I say, you knew him best of all the

205

people we interviewed. Even more than his father, I suspect. There might be something you can tell me that I overlooked at the time. I'm just looking to tie up all the loose ends, Mr Taylor. Not as a cop. But as someone looking to bring peace of mind to the people that Alex hurt.'

He hesitated. 'I have somewhere to be,' he said. 'My mother ... it's her birthday. We have ... she'll be ... She gets upset if I'm late.'

'I know how it is.'

He smiled. No humour there. Perhaps a kind of sadness. 'I'm sure you don't.'

'Then we'll talk later.'

'You won't let this go?'

'I'm tenacious,' I said, 'because my clients pay me to be that way.'

He nodded. Again, his head ticked from side to side. A metronome in a lanky wig. 'Fine,' he said. 'We can talk. But the minute I don't like your questions, I'm walking.'

'Fair enough,' I said.

I watched as he got into his car.

Trying to search for any sign that I'd shaken him.

The closest cafe was a Costa Coffee at the local Tesco. Around us, shoppers bustled and echoed from the aisles and the coffee machine provided a discordant, hissing, steaming soundtrack.

We both drank black coffees – Americanos,

206

the barista had insisted when we ordered – and for a few moments we had nothing to say to each other. An awkward and unexpected blind first date. We both struggled to find a way to break the ice.

Finally: 'What were you afraid he would say?'

Taylor sipped at his coffee. When he swallowed, his Adam's apple bobbed up and down. It was prominent in his neck, more than you'd have noticed in the photograph he had on the company website, and when he got nervous about what he was saying, it bobbed so hard you worried it might dislodge itself and spit halfway across the room.

'I was afraid that he wouldn't be the man I used to think he was,' said Taylor. 'It's one thing to know what he did, to find the evidence, to work in his office without him there. But to face him again, knowing what I knew...' He bowed his head, looking away from me. 'I couldn't ... How could you know everything you'd been through with this person and then have to come to terms with them doing something like that? I couldn't ... I didn't want. I didn't want to remember him as a monster. To me, I wanted to think of it like, like maybe he'd died, you know?' He finally looked up again. It couldn't have been any more convincing if there were tears in his eyes. But there weren't. He wasn't playing it up like that.

Maybe that was meant to make it more convincing.

But like I say, there are things you're looking for that are outside the normal reactions, the things that maybe you can't put a name to, but that you know are there. Small gestures or changes that you only notice with experience.

'You were his friend. You shared a flat with him during your student days. You probably knew him better than most. There was no sign of unusual behaviour?'

'Define unusual. We were geeks, Mr McNee. Unusual goes with the territory. Especially at that age. I just ... when you think about those other children ... If I'd known at the time, seen the way he looked at them...'

Playing it up just a little too much.

'The other children? The ones that Amityville connected to Moorehead?'

Taylor nodded. Suddenly reticent. His words and his act drying up like spit on a hotplate. He licked his lips. Playing for time.

Had he meant to bring up those other children?

Had he taken this act too far?

He had never commented publicly on the other children that Moorehead had been linked to. The media had tried to get him to speak, but he never said anything. Everyone took this as his way of cutting his time with Moorehead out of his life completely.

But was it something else?

'If you'd seen something at the time? You weren't living at the same address during those years.'

'We were still friends. I would visit him, sometimes.' Speaking a little too fast. Eyes looking to the side, not meeting mine. Slight sheen of sweat on his lips and forehead.

He was a liar. Covering something up. And I needed to know what it was.

It could have been a tiny thing. An omission he now regretted or perhaps a suspicion he'd never acted on. Or it could be bigger. A secret that would finally help me understand the inconsistencies in Alex Moorehead, the man who admitted killing one child and denied all the others that followed his established MO.

If Taylor's cover-up was as big as I suspected, then it had helped put away an innocent man before finally killing him. By inches. If he was innocent, then Alex Moorehead's suicide was maybe less of a tragedy than if he'd continued living with the consequences of one man's deception.

Was Moorehead's death a release?

Not the final escape of a murderer but of an innocent man?

The problem with Taylor was that if he was lying, he probably believed his own deception. The consequences of telling a lie for so long: you start to behave as though it's the truth.

So how could I draw him out, make him admit to a truth I could only guess at?

I needed to find the cracks in his deception, the places where his lie was at its weakest, where even he could see the seams and understand the fraud.

I hated to do it.

I didn't want to do it.

But I needed to.

TWENTY-EIGHT

I took a walk down to the water, breathed in the air. Gulls circled, occasionally looping down, grabbing any fish that came too close to the surface. At the beach, the waves broke gently against the sand.

I couldn't shake the feeling that Taylor was lying. I needed to find that chink in his armour, work in my knife.

My interrogative strengths had always been psychological, getting people to reveal the truth of who they were. It had been an instinctual thing at first, but I had worked on it over the years. Physical intimidation had never been my preferred tactic.

When I moved over to the private side, I discovered the need to understand my clients more than I ever had a suspect in interview. Police work always had a straightforward goal, an end in sight. You were working to put away the criminals and protect the innocent. But working for private clients meant digging through grey motivations and the silent ethical realities that they brought into the office. People often glossed over the real reasons for hiring a private detective. I had frequently had as much trouble with my own clients as I ever had with a suspect.

I had come to believe that – to some degree at least – Alex Moorehead was innocent. So, I was looking for someone who could give me the answers as to why he would take the rap for something he never did. I was looking for the one-armed man, like Dr Henry Kimble. Except I couldn't be certain that there ever really had been one.

Taylor had answers. I was sure of it. But were they the answers I wanted?

In the back of my mind there were suspicions and conspiracy theories too wild to say out loud. The Wood connection had me worried. Taylor was hiding something. I knew the kind of pressure the ex-assistant chief constable had exerted on people. I'd had to fight to bring to the surface the terrible things he'd done.

Taylor had fitted up his friend. I was sure of it.

But why?

On whose authority?

I watched the gulls for a while, let the breeze caress my face. I caught the scent of salt whipped off the water. The sound of the waves and the call of the birds made me feel a million miles away from civilization.

I wondered if I was just being paranoid. Becoming a conspiracy theorist; seeing connections where none existed, making up stories to fit facts I had already decided upon.

Nearby, kids shouted to each other. Their voices were rough, less innocent than I remembered being at that age. But then this was a harsh world we had created. Our own fears created a generation who frightened us because we'd given them more knowledge than they'd ever be ready for, without the critical tools to deal with it. These kids had been brought up in the spectre of dead children whose cases were highly publicized, pushed to the forefront of the public's mind. They were a generation in constant fear. Which made them harder than any generation before. They'd developed tough skins to deal with the fear their parents subjected them to every day. My last couple of months on the force, I remember thinking that the juvenile crimes were getting worse than the adult ones. That there was a generation who'd been brought up with both the fear of the bogey-man and the certainty that they themselves were invincible, that they could do whatever they liked and still get away with it.

Thinking like that made me feel old, out of touch. An old man in his mid-thirties. Worried for the youth of today, his own childhood lost in the dim and distant past.

As I turned to walk back into town, where

I'd left the car, one of the kids – couldn't have been older than ten or eleven – shouted at me as his gang came into earshot: 'Oy, mister! Got any fags on you?'

I shook my head, walked on.

'Fuck you, then!' he shouted.

'Paedo!' another yelled, no sense of what the word really meant. Or the terrors and nightmares that it would give his mother.

No evidence of sexual assault.

Back at the office, I read and re-read the reports concerning Justin Farnham's death. He'd been murdered. Tortured, even. But not sexually interfered with.

That still jarred with what we found on Moorehead's PC. The pictures had been brutal, all with a twisted sexual element. And yet Moorehead himself showed no other signs of sexual interest in children.

At the time it had been easy to explain his inability to carry through the act with Justin, resorting instead to the violence that existed in the second half of the equation. He wasn't ready to cross the line between fantasy and reality, but in starting his crime he had to ensure that there were no witnesses. But in jail, he'd seen numerous counsellors and never once – aside from some vague mumbling around the issue – had he expressed or displayed that kind of pathology.

And besides, Project Amityville later linked

other, earlier, cases to Alex. The other murder providing a definite sense of a killer escalating towards sexual gratification. Given Justin's position in the timelines of these murders, there should have been a more sexual component to the murder; a hint of escalation.

So why the apparent disconnect between crime and killer?

I called Bobby Soren. On his unlisted number, of course.

Soren was also known as 'the Grinch', a paranoid computer hacker who saw himself as the online Banksy. He'd been arrested and fined a few times, suspected and glowered at several more but mostly no one knew who he was, because he was too damn good at covering his tracks.

'Awright, McNee,' he said when he realized it was me on the other end of the line. 'How's it hanging, my man? Little to the left?'

I didn't even bother answering. 'Need your help, Bobby.'

'Aye, aye,' he said. 'Hugg E-bear, that's me.'

It was a good gag by his standards, even putting the emphasis in the right places.

'How are you on history?'

'I remember something from school 'bout a Schlieffen Plan, but only 'cos it sounded cool.'

'I mean old computers.'

'How old?'

'2004, 2005,' I said. 'Around then, any-way.'

'Aye, aye,' he said. 'Real old, then.'

'Real old.'

'Know how old I was then?'

'How old?'

'Still shiteing my breeks is how old,' he said. And laughed. 'But, sure, I could prob-ably still have taken apart those old bad boys and put 'em back together. Strong, faster, better.' Bobby had a thing about TV shows from decades before he was born. Ripped them from online streams, watched them over and over. *Starsky and Hutch* was his favourite, but clearly he'd been watching Lee Majors in the *Six Million Dollar Man* lately.

'You want to meet?' I asked.

'I got time,' he said. 'If you've got the good stuff.'

'Aye,' I said. 'I've got the good stuff.'

Soren was an odd mix of clichés. Dressed like a proto-nerd with ill-fitting white track-suit and baseball cap with over-sized peak, but living the life of your typical alpha-geek, existing on an odd diet of sugared drinks and junk food.

The good stuff, for Soren, was a multi-pack of Red Bull and several oversized bags of M&Ms.

We met at a coffee house in the town centre. The Empire, trying to pretend like it was a slice of New York in the centre of Dundee. Maybe you could fool yourself if you didn't look outside. Or listen to the accents.

I ordered a black coffee. No one insisted on calling it an Americano. Soren had a Coke. Occasionally, he stroked the goodie bag I'd brought. When he noticed me looking at him, he laughed and said, 'My preccioussss,' in his best Gollum voice.

'I looked into it,' he said. 'What you said. It'd be piss easy to hack into someone's old PC and plant a trail. More so back then because people weren't quite so sophisticated when it came to looking out for hackers' footprints, know what I mean? Now you need to be better than the best because the cops, they all hire the best to watch out for guys like me.'

'You never fancied working as a police geek?'

'Fuck the man,' he said, a little too loudly and punched his fist in the air. Several people looked round. I tried not to look back in case I found myself having to apologize for my companion's behaviour. He leaned forward, as though sharing a deep, dark secret, voice suddenly sotto: 'They'd never have me, anyway. Not now.'

I couldn't argue. A few years back, the Grinch had hacked Tayside Police's website and replaced the homepage with an animation of a copper humping a pig. Political subtlety wasn't really his strong point. Staying off the grid, however, was.

'So it would be possible to add images to a hard drive, make it look like they'd been there a long time, maybe even redirect where they came from?'

'Back then? Oh, aye. It was possible. Security being what it was, then, the hackers were always one step ahead of everyone else.'

I thought about it for a minute. Figured the Grinch was probably now the equivalent of what Alex Moorehead had been then. So why didn't Moorehead even float the possibility that someone had added those pictures to his drive? At the very least it would have been a good delay tactic while we investigated the possibility. Allowed him to sort his thoughts and his alibi.

Was I clutching out in desperation, eyes closed, fingers hoping that whatever they touched would help pull me out of the dark?

Soren said, 'Deep in thought, man?'

'Just ... considering things.'

'You have something you want me to take a look at?'

'Nah,' I said. 'Wish I bloody did, though.' If Soren could take a look, maybe he could apply over six years' worth of experience with computers since the original hack and uncover something that whoever planted those images didn't realize they had left behind.

A grand plan. Except the computer was stored away in an old evidence locker somewhere. If anyone even knew where that was, it was still going to be impossible for me to get to.

After all, I had no real friends left on the force. At least, none who would be willing to stick their neck out.

TWENTY-NINE

The warehouse was even more desolate than it had been eighteen months earlier. If it was dying before, there was no trace of a heartbeat now.

An air of tragedy continued to hang over the building. Even the birds gave it a wide berth. A couple of lone gulls sat on the low wall that marked the boundaries of the long-empty industrial estate and stared at me, as though they couldn't work out what anyone would be doing here.

Except making a point. A childish point.

But it was too late to change my mind. When I spoke to Griggs, this was the address I gave him. He hadn't questioned my decision, and I wonder if he understood the significance. If he didn't, then Susan certainly would.

The car, when it pulled up, was a late-model BMW. An old joke about managers driving BMWs because it's the only car they can spell skittered through my brain.

Griggs got out of the driver's side, regulation suit and dark military-style jacket, may-

220

be thinking he looked like something out of *The X-Files*. I noticed the passenger door open as well. My breath caught in my throat. Susan got out, dressed in a dark jacket that went down to just below her knees, and dark boots that hugged her calves.

They walked towards me. I stayed where I was. The birds scattered, steering clear of the warehouse. Like I said, they must have sensed what happened here. And maybe had an idea of what might happen now.

When he got close enough, Griggs said, 'You want to talk? Seeing sense, at last?'

I looked past him to Susan. Her eyes told me everything I needed to know. Susan had always been her father's daughter, and she had inherited his ability to play her cards close to her chest. But some things you can't hide. Some things are too personal to disguise. Especially from someone who knows you too well.

Griggs turned from me to look at her and then back again. He said, 'You're trying to make a point.'

'I don't know what you mean.'

Susan stepped forward. 'I didn't think you still had this in you,' she said. 'But OK, I get it. I hurt your feelings. You wanted to hurt me back...'

I shook my head. 'It just seemed ... no one comes here. No one will know we met here.'

'You're a bastard, McNee,' she said. 'You

have always had that in you, but...'

'This is a beautiful reunion,' said Griggs, 'but we're freezing our bollocks off out here and I need to know this was about more than just petty revenge.'

I nodded. 'Aye,' I said. 'It is.'

'You're accepting my offer?'

'Maybe.'

'Maybe?'

'I have conditions.'

'For fuck's—'

'Hear me out,' I said. 'It's not about money or anything else. It's that you give me some breathing space. You make these charges go away. Let me find another way to get on that old bastard's side.'

'How? This is time sensitive, McNee.'

'Family's important to him. Not just his own. The whole idea. Those pictures you showed me ... he doted on that child. He thinks of himself as one of the good guys. Compartmentalizes his business decisions from his apparent ethical beliefs. I can use this case to get close to him. And then ... I think I can show him that we're on the same side.'

'Want to tell me how?' Griggs asked.

'No,' I said. 'There's no time. But it's ... Look, Susan, you know you can trust me. I've done a lot of stupid things, but my word still means something. Right?'

Maybe it was the wrong choice of words

given everything that had happened between us. She looked away for a moment, and I thought I saw her lips move, but any words were lifted and carried by the wind so that no one would ever know what they were.

She turned to Griggs and said, flat, 'It might be our best chance.'

Griggs nodded. Turned back to me. 'OK, McNee,' he said. 'Fair enough. Tell me what you want. Let's haggle for justice.'

The duty officer glared at me, but didn't say anything as we packed up the evidence and Griggs signed the appropriate forms. I did as I'd been told and hung back. Keeping quiet because anything I could say would only cause difficulties. Griggs was bending enough rules as it was without being accused of assisting one of the most notorious pains-in-the-arse Tayside Police had ever known, on or off the job.

When we got back to my offices, Soren was chatting away to Dot like they were old friends, devouring cups of milky tea faster than she could boil the kettle. Mostly, though, she ignored him, so the friendly conversation was one sided. When I came in, she raised her head and looked at me over her reading glasses. I ushered Soren through to my office and shut the door. Thought maybe I could hear her sigh of relief from outside.

Griggs placed the computer on my desk

and unwrapped it. Soren regarded him with suspicion. 'Anything I do,' Soren said, 'is with your permission, right? You can't touch me for—'

'He's not interested in you,' I said.

Griggs regarded the smaller man for a moment and said, 'Today.'

Soren grinned. His incisors were sharp and whiter than you'd expect given the junk he shoved down his gullet. He got himself set up. Laughed as he sorted the cables and attached the old machine to one of my flat-screen monitors. 'Anyone got ten minutes while this old heap boots?' he asked.

While he busied himself, I put the kettle on. Griggs joined me in the far corner of the office. 'This had better be worth it for you,' he said. 'Because right now it feels like a big joke at my expense.'

'I'm a man of my word.'

He nodded.

When Soren was done, Sandy and I stood back, watched the master at work. He giggled with delight at how long it took him to complete basic tasks, and I had to admit it was startling to see what had once been a state-of-the-art machine measure up to the convenience we've come to expect from to-day's PCs. Six years was a long time in com-puting terms. I had assumed it would be only a difference of seconds but it was more often like minutes, the wait for any task to be completed.

The minutes stretched to hours. Dot brought us some take out and then left for the evening. For a while, I went out and read a book in the reception area.

Finally, Soren had something to tell us.

'The images are still there. I don't want to look at that shite and I hope you don't either. Fucksakes, if it's anything like what you said... . my limit's *Two Girls One Cup*, know what I mean?'

Sadly, I did. But didn't let on.

'Right,' he said after a moment or two, looking oddly disappointed, like maybe he'd expected a laugh or a moment of recognition. But he wasn't going to get it. This was serious business. Even he could sense that. 'So. The pictures. First glance, aye, it looks like they were downloaded from mirror sites. A glance at his internet history confirms where he went to find this nasty shite. So it all looks kosher.'

'Sorry,' Griggs said to me. 'I don't know what else you were expecting to—'

'Hoy-oy,' Soren said. 'Calm the ham, man. Calm the fuckin' ham. This shite is not what it appears to be. It's like fuckin' *Transformers*. The good shit, I mean. None of that Michael Bay fuck-the-frame bollocks. More than meets the eye is what I'm saying. There's code underneath. Hidden deep. Someone tried to redirect where we were looking.

225

Because the problem we have is that these images were not downloaded to this fucking PC. They were downloaded elsewhere and transferred. Someone just tried – and did a good job, too – to make it look like the downloads originated from this wee clapped-out bugger's IP address. If you weren't looking for anything sus, you probably wouldn't notice.' He smiled and gently patted the 3.5in. floppy drive on the front of the old tower. 'Probably the files were introduced through this little beauty.' He did the same to the 10x CD-ROM drive. 'Or this one. Christ, doesn't it say something, eh? No one worries about CD speed any more. And floppys? Fucking forget it. Obsolete is not the word, man.'

Griggs said, 'To me it's still cutting-edge.'

Soren didn't say anything, but curled his upper lip in something like a snarl.

'Anyway, man, the point is that this shite was downloaded on another machine and then transferred over. And they've been interfered with. They look all right on the surface, but you go deeper, you can see someone's interfered with them. If you know what you're looking for. If you're expecting to find someone fucking about. Which I did. Because why else would you call on me?'

'Do you know when this happened?'

'They were all placed on the same date, I can tell you that.'

226

None of this had come up before. If Jason Taylor was as good as he had claimed, surely he would have noticed that the images had been interfered with. The incriminating evidence had been the fact that some of the lesser images – those blurred snapshots of anonymous children clearly taken without consent in public places – were associated with the model number of a camera that Moorehead owned. Another fake?

Whoever did it was determined to make us think that Moorehead had downloaded these files himself. Combine with his initial silence regarding Justin Farnham, and you had all the makings of a guilty man.

'So tell me,' I said. 'Clear as you can. What all of this means.'

He did. Griggs and I turned to look at each other. Despite what the added code tried to claim, the modified files – including those that included the damning evidence against Moorehead – had been placed on Moorehead's PC several days, maybe weeks, after Justin Farnham's body had been found. Meaning the investigation had been messed with from the start. Meaning that someone had tried their hardest to make it look like Moorehead was guilty. And, like the Keystone Cops we were, we'd fallen for it.

Hook.

Line.

Sinker.

THIRTY

What I now knew:

1) Jason Taylor had been present during at least one of the disappearances, visiting his old friend Alex Moorehead. He hadn't mentioned specifics, but it was plausible that he had been in the area on or around the time of Farnham's disappearance. Which would also explain why he was so ready and able to assist in the investigation.

2) Someone had planted the images on Moorehead's drive the day that Justin Farnham disappeared. Someone with not inconsiderable computing knowledge.

If the Grinch could see the fakery, why had Taylor missed it?

What's two plus two?

Taylor had the skills to pull off the hack that Soren uncovered. The opportunity, too. And I still wasn't happy with how he behaved when anyone brought up his old friend's alleged crimes. He was oddball enough, but there was something hinky about his reaction to my approach.

Griggs gave me three more days on the

case. He didn't think that this would get me any closer to David Burns. But I knew that if I could make Burns feel I had achieved something he could not – justice for the mothers who had lost their sons – then it would go some way to smoothing my path to his inner circle. A less obvious route than the one proposed by Griggs, establishing the kind of bona-fides that would be hard to fake by any undercover officer.

But Griggs wasn't convinced. He wasn't convinced I was right about Taylor. And that was the least of his concerns. Nevertheless, he was giving me three days before allowing Kellen to follow her instincts on the charges against me.

Call that generous.

At least it was enough time to breathe. At the very least to come up with a new plan of action.

I called Jason Taylor, told him I had some more questions. Assured him this would be the last time we talked.

He hesitated. Said he'd talked to his mother about this, and she'd made the point that what I was doing could be seen as harassment.

I told him that this was not harassment. That I was merely looking for more background detail. That if he didn't talk to me, it was likely other people would be coming around with questions in the next few months. With the papers already running stories about Moorehead's death, how long would it be until someone remembered his name again?

He relented eventually. But there was still a reluctance about him. Maybe that was understandable.

Once we were done, I figured on checking Taylor's family. Twice now he'd mentioned his mother during conversations. Maybe just because it was her birthday, but there had been an odd emphasis in the way he mentioned her that set alarm bells off in the back of my brain.

I dug deeper. With his full name, address and business details, it was easier to root further into the system, using back channels to get information on his extended family. It's a little like researching a family tree, but the emphasis is not on reaching as far back as possible, but getting the maximum information on each person involved.

Which was why I was surprised to find my search stopping early.

Jason Taylor's mother was dead.

Her birthday was when he said it was, but she'd been dead for thirteen years.

Thirteen years.

The number felt familiar.

Thirteen years.

I pulled up the files on the Moorehead murders. Everything I had on the project that Wemyss had been running. All the Disappeared. All the evidence – however tenuous – that linked them to the Farnham murder and to Moorehead in particular.

Thirteen years.

The first death. The first child to die. Andrew Peterson. Ten years old. Body found in the Tay maybe five or six miles from his home. It had been death by misadventure until the post-mortem ruled that the injuries which killed Andrew could not have been sustained accidentally. By the time anyone realized this, of course, the trail was cold. Andrew had been dead for a week when they found him. Any evidence destroyed by his immersion in the water and exposure to the elements.

But the dates matched with Alex Moorehead living two streets away. Had Jason Taylor called in to visit his old friend? Or was I looking too hard for something that was never there?

Still, it gave me something to work with.

I called Fife police, talked to the duty sergeant, asked if there had been any word regarding Alex Moorehead's father. He told me, in so many words, to go fuck myself.

I put in a request with the council for more information regarding Mrs Taylor's death. Knew that it would be put in a queue, that I probably wouldn't get the information I was looking for until the next day.

That was fine.

It was enough to know he had lied to me, or at least tried to steer me wrong during our conversation. That could prove enough to give me an advantage, to help trip him up.

That night, I slept soundly, but when I woke up in the morning, there was a strange sensation in the pit of my stomach. I had managed to knock all the pillows off the bed while I was asleep, and was wrapped up in a mess of blankets that clung to the sweat of my body.

I showered and shaved, heated up some porridge oats in the microwave and wolfed them down. The coffee helped a little, too, and an hour later when I looked at myself in the mirror, I resembled a normal human being. Vaguely.

My meeting with Taylor was at 2 p.m. It was only just past seven. I killed time running over everything that I had, ensuring there were no gaps in my logic. Today, I planned to twist the knife, to see whether I could get him to admit the secret he was hiding.

Maybe it was a leap, I admit, to think that Taylor was guilty. So far what I had was a coincidence of timing. But who else would have the means to frame Alex so completely? Not his father, certainly. And then there was the coincidence of his mother's death timing so well with the first child to disappear. And the look in Taylor's eyes when he had mentioned a woman who had been dead for thirteen years.

All I had were suppositions and questions. I was focused on Taylor, but other questions needed answering. This time around no one would be left uncertain about the truth, and for once, there would be no loose ends. No questions to be asked.

Just the simple truth.

If I was right in my suppositions, I still had to know two things.

Where was Alex's father?

What happened to him after he talked to his son?

There was taking some time to get your head around something and then there was simply vanishing off the face of the earth.

Hardly the stuff that High Court cases are built from. But then I wasn't a police officer any more. I was a private citizen. There were things I could do that I would have never even considered as a policeman.

I just hoped I didn't have to find out what they were.

Jason Taylor's house, ten minutes outside Ayr, was an anachronistically modern monstrosity that only a small fortune could build. It stood on a gentle hill, overlooking the town on one side and the water on the other. In the summer it might have been oddly beautiful, but with autumn fast ending the building – glass and steel and angles – looked cold and impersonal. Hardly where you'd seek warmth in the winter months.

When Taylor met me at the front door, he shook my hand. 'I got lucky. An aunt I never knew I had passed away.'

'This was built in her memory?'

I didn't mention his mother. Keeping that for the sucker punch.

He smiled, his lips pressing together, and his eyes as cold and impersonal as his house. He said, 'Come in, please. Don't take it personally, but I hope you don't become a regular visitor.'

I didn't say anything, followed him inside.

The house was a property developer's wet dream. Built before the recession, I had to guess, it was all open plan and white space. The high windows stretched from ceiling to floor. There was no sign of it actually being lived in. No sneaky stains waiting to be cleaned. No clothes tossed on chairs or books discarded. It was a show house. The word *mausoleum* crept into my brain and bounced around.

He led me to what I assumed was the living area, designated more by the furniture than walls or doors. The flat-screen TV was placed at an odd angle, the real focus on those windows that looked out towards the water.

'It has to cost you in window-cleaning bills,' I said.

'Self-cleaning,' he replied. His tone implied that it should have been obvious.

'I usually just let the rain do the job for me,' I said.

Again that tight-lipped expression that might have passed for a smile.

We sat on white-leather sofas, facing each other. A coffee table separated us. The table was low, with a pine frame and glass top. I wondered if it was self-cleaning like the double glazing. I wondered just how much the aunt had left him.

'How long have you been here?'

'Five years, give or take.'

'A change from your student days,' I said. 'Sharing grubby little flats with Alex.'

'I can't be held responsible for his actions.' He thought this over for a moment. 'If that's what you're implying.'

'I'm sorry,' I said. 'I don't mean to treat you like the enemy. Guess it was all those years being a policeman. You sit down to have a chat with someone, you start treating them like a suspect.'

'Even when they're not accused of anything? Even when they're the ones who helped you break the case?'

I shrugged. 'Even then.'

'You want a drink?' He stood up. The leather of his sofa creaked gently. 'Coffee, perhaps?'

'Nothing stronger,' I said. 'I'm driving, after all.'

He nodded and walked away. I couldn't see the kitchen, despite the open plan. He disappeared behind a jutting wall somewhere. Of course, I had yet to work out where he slept or even worked. I looked around, and saw one of the walls had a bookcase embedded. There were very few books. In fact, there were none. Just some ornaments and a few DVDs and Blu-Rays. Mostly blockbusters. Big-budget studio fare that didn't demand much in the way of thought; the kind of movies sold on star names rather than compelling drama. Looking back at the TV, I noticed that while it didn't dominate, it was still an impressive size.

I heard footsteps, looked round and saw Taylor come back carrying two white mugs. I said, 'Not a reader?'

'I have books.'

'Just not here.'

'In my study,' he said. 'Mostly for work, you know. Maybe I should read, but there's just so much else to distract us these days.'

'Sure,' I said. 'Like flashy websites and sparkling social-media feeds.'

'You're not a man who likes the modern world.'

'It's fine by me,' I said. 'I just think some people need to look beyond the immediate gratification offered by modern technology.'

'I've heard it can be addictive.'

'Once you realize you can find anything you need online,' I said, 'who has time for books?'

'*Reductio ad absurdum*,' he said. 'About the only Latin I know. I think you're mocking me, Mr McNee. Not a good start to our new friendship.'

'I'm sorry.' I reached out and took the coffee from him. I lifted it to my face. The heat made me think of when I was a boy and my mother got rid of colds by placing my head under a wet towel and over a bowl of steaming hot water.

We sat down again.

'What do you want to talk about, Mr McNee?'

'The past.'

He shook his head. 'Everything you could want to know is in the files, surely.'

'Not everything.'

'Right.'

'Tell me about DCI Wood.'

'Who?'

'The man who brought you on board, Jason. The detective who called you in because he believed you could do what the techies couldn't.'

'Aye, right. Him.' Jason laughed. It wasn't natural. 'Aye, I remember him, all right. Friend of a friend, you know?'

'No.'

'His daughter. We went to college together.'

'He knew about the Moorehead connection?'

'Alex didn't know her so well. I mean, she'd know the name, I guess. Me and Alex being friends like we were. But Alex was a homebody, liked to spend his time indoors, know what I mean? Most of the time other people ... he didn't like them.'

'And you did?'

'Wasn't a party animal, like. But—'

I nodded. It was enough to cut him off.

'Alex was odd. Always. And, Mr McNee, don't think I don't know what you're implying...'

'What am I implying?'

'That the recently deceased Deputy Chief Constable Wood was somehow responsible for what happened to Alex. And that I was complicit.'

It wasn't like I was being overly subtle, I suppose. 'Well?'

'Sorry to disappoint.' He smiled. Unpleasant and unnatural. 'There's no conspiracy. He brought me in because he knew who I was. Before that, we had no contact. After that, I never talked to him again. Frankly, I thought he was a bit of a wanker.'

'That right?'

'Aye.'

238

The same way you develop instincts for detecting lies, you also get the feeling when someone's telling you the truth. Jason Taylor may have been lying about his feelings for his old friend Alex, but I got the impression he was telling the truth about Wood. The moment we started talking about the corrupt old fucker, Taylor's body language had relaxed considerably. I had lost the scent of his deception, and he knew it.

So if I was wrong about Wood, was I wrong about anything else?

I said, 'So if you weren't coerced, tell me why you turned on your friend?'

'He was a pervert.'

'You didn't know that before you found those images.' I had to wonder what kind of friend would deliberately seek out evidence to implicate his buddy in any crime. Surely he would have been looking to prove Moorehead's innocence?

All the poise and suave he liked to project vanished for just a moment, revealing what I'd seen before; a man trying to hide his own secrets.

'Tell me how you knew. Because when you were brought on board, no one knew about the images. All they knew was that a child was dead.'

'I ... it was ... the situation. That was ... I mean, your boss said it, right? That DI?'

'Bright. His name was Ernie Bright.'

'Sure. Right. That's the one. He said it. He said that the way Alex found the body was … too easy. Too much of a coincidence. I agreed with him. And there were other things, too. Just set off warning bells.'

'OK,' I said. 'Then tell me about Alex.'

'What about him?'

'Oh,' I said. 'How about everything?'

THIRTY-ONE

Alex Moorehead was a genius.

He was also introverted, uncertain, prone to panic attacks and convinced that he would be proved wrong in spectacular fashion. About everything.

This, at least, according to Jason Taylor.

'He had this fear that one day he would just forget everything he knew about computers. The one thing he believed made him special would just vanish. Or worse, people would realize it had never been there in the first place.'

They met on the second day of term. They stayed at the same halls, and were often, at half-past two in the morning, the only two people left in the computing lab working on something most of their classmates wouldn't understand even by graduation.

They were bona-fide geeks.

'I'm not sure Alex even had a proper girlfriend at school,' Taylor said in a way I wasn't sure was meant to be a joke.

Taylor didn't have half the smarts of his new friend. He understood that even then.

But Taylor was the one with the business sense, the one with the ambition. 'You meet a genius,' he told me, 'and if the first thing you think isn't, how can I make money off this guy, then you're an idiot.'

But their friendship wasn't simple utilitarianism. Taylor grew to like the shy, introverted geek. Over the course of the next few months, they spent more and more time together. They shared a love of kung-fu flicks on dodgy VHS import and the kind of hair rock that must have seemed at odds with their button-down appearance.

'Sounds odd,' he told me, 'but it's true.'

They started planning for the future. Designed programs riffing off their favourite games. 'We had this idea for a Doom rip-off,' he said. 'It was pretty good, but you know how things are at that age. We had all these half-finished projects that never really went anywhere.'

The big one, though, was anti-virus software. 'Security's big in computing,' Taylor told me. 'Always has been, always will be. Data is commerce online, and you can never be too careful about what you do with that data, whether it's your own or a client's. The system we designed was supposed to be this dynamic, self-propagating security system that dealt intelligently with threats, constantly encrypted secure data and generally did what your standard AV does with the added bonus that it really learned how to protect itself.'

Sounded good to me. But apparently there were issues with the cost of the software and upkeep that stopped the project from becoming a real business proposition.

In the end Taylor went down south, worked for a few game-development companies and finally started Redboot. But Alex, so Taylor said, never seemed too worried about going beyond the border. He worked for several Scottish start-ups before drifting into IT repair.

'All that genius going to waste,' Taylor said. He seemed genuinely to regret what happened. 'Bloody shame, really. He could have done anything, but he never had the confidence.'

All of this tallied with what he said the first time around. I had read his statements. Hearing the way he told the story, however, it came across as too smooth. Thought through. Practised.

How had it sounded the first time? Not written down and captured on the page, but witnessed in an interview room by two senior coppers.

'So what about all those plans you had together? What about using him to earn yourself some serious cash?'

'The other problem with geniuses,' he said, 'is that they're not as focused as you think they'd be. Try getting him to do anything he didn't want to do? Like coaxing a five-year-old to eat their greens.' He smiled, then. Something bashful in the smile that I didn't really understand. 'He wanted to do his own thing, and every time I had a sound idea, he'd laugh it off.'

But they remained friends. Good friends. They'd meet up every few months, drink a bit too much, maybe break out some hair records and talk TV and comics. 'We were geeks,' he said. 'I know we were. The kind of guys who never really grow up.' He was silent for a second, and seemed to consider something. 'I wonder ... I mean, if that had something to do with what he did. The fact that he never really grew up...'

I shook my head. 'The geeks are the geeks,' I said. 'They tend not to be violent or psychopathic.'

'Despite what the *Daily Mail* says about computer games players?'

'Sure,' I said. 'Despite that.'

But something was rattling inside my head: the kind of guys who never really grow up.

I was thinking about his mother. His apparent devotion to her so many years after her death. The fact he talked about her as though she was still alive.

Taylor told me how he started to worry about Alex. How every time they saw each other, it became clear that Alex was becoming more removed from the world around him. 'He was never really a guy for making friends, but that became more and more pronounced. At least at work. He always seemed to get on well with his neighbours,' Taylor said.

He hesitated, then. As though realizing what he'd just said.

I was getting Oscar-nomination vibes from Taylor. Like I'd suspected before, this was an act. He was trying to lead me somewhere.

Same trick he'd pulled all those years ago?

It should have been my first major investigation. Ernie had been in charge, sure, but he'd involved me as much as possible. He'd run every theory past me, made sure I sat in on the interviews. I was as responsible as Ernie for any mistakes that had been made.

And then, at the critical moment, I had been invalided out. The car crash that sent my whole life off course also impacted the investigation. The loss of an investigating officer and the substitution of a man who was clearly looking to clear the case as quickly as possible so he could return to the politicking that was taking him to the top had meant that the investigation lost its focus. Although it appeared to regain it, I had to wonder if perhaps someone had been able to push it in a direction that suited their own needs.

Ernie and Wood had overlooked Taylor.

Not just because of Wood's personal connection to the IT geek, but because he gently nudged them towards Moorehead using what I now knew to be planted evidence, and the smooth story that he recounted about how awkward their suspect was, how there was always something a little different about Alex Moorehead.

Taylor hadn't been dumb enough to push his point too far. He'd made the crack about how well Alex had got on with the neighbours wherever he went, left that to bounce around the brain, do the hard work for him.

But this wasn't nearly six years ago. I wasn't an eager-to-please detective in training. Nor was I a cop who'd already found a near-perfect suspect.

Did Taylor know I was on to him? That I was seeing through his lies?

He'd be dumb not to have realized. And he hadn't got away with what he'd done for all these years by being an idiot.

Most criminals are caught because of a simple, idiotic mistake.

The Yorkshire Ripper on a traffic violation. Al Capone on tax evasion. Your basic burglar staying in the house for too long or not checking that someone's home.

So far Jason Taylor had stayed under the radar.

And I still couldn't be sure that I wasn't imprinting motivation on to him. That he wasn't just a socially awkward IT geek, same way I believed Moorehead had been. Sure, Taylor was more polished and presentable, but you can learn that kind of behaviour if you apply yourself. The self-help publishing industry is built entirely on that premise.

How to Win Friends and Influence People.
Be All You Can Be.
Face The Fear (And Do It Anyway).

If Taylor really did have books in this impersonal white space of a home, then those would be the titles I expected to find alongside all the technical documentation and geek-speak bibles.

I said, 'You were there, at his home, on or around at least two of the occasions when a child went missing. You told me so yourself.' I had double-checked dates and times. Read witness statements. Gone over all the case notes. When asked about Moorehead's social life, people had said he was a quiet man, but always there was the mention of a friend who came to stay every so often. Never named. Never questioned.

But it had to have been Jason Taylor.

He swallowed. The blood drained from his face just enough for me to see he was nervous, but no more so than any individual facing an unwarranted accusation. Still not enough. Right now I was merely probing with the knife, running it along the surface of his armour, gently prodding to find that chink before driving the blade home.

Ernie used to say, '*You need to be sure what the suspect will say. You need to be convinced of their motivations, of what they did. If you aren't one hundred per cent sure and you twist that knife, then you can send an innocent man down.*'

But that was always a possibility.

'I realize that, now. It's not like we were with each other twenty-four hours a day. I just...'

'You must have seen something,' I said. 'In his behaviour. I'm not a psychologist, but I know something about pattern killers.'

'You don't call them serial?'

'It depends who you talk to,' I said. 'I'm no psychologist, like I said.'

'There's spree killers, too,' Taylor said. His tone breathless. He had a theme, was desperate to change the subject. 'There's something about them ... they kill lots of people, but only during one incident. Like ... that guy ... Dunblane.'

I nodded.

The Dunblane massacre, in 1996, had shocked the nation. A terrible affair; ex-army guy snapping and walking into a primary school with four handguns. That one incident was all it took for the police to crack down on handgun usage. The government took decisive action to prevent further tragedy. It didn't stop handgun use altogether, but it had a clear effect on the populace and our attitude to weapons.

Of course, if the government really wanted to clamp down on dangerous weapons in Scotland, they'd call an amnesty on pint glasses. They had been the number one cause of serious injury that I'd seen during my years as a beat copper. Saturday nights, a bit of bevvy, and people lost all control.

But the idea of something like Dunblane happening again was too much to contemplate.

'Maybe he was just used to the idea of killing,' Taylor said, talking about Alex Moorehead again. 'Maybe it didn't affect him outwardly. Like ... like the way you don't think when you crack open another bottle of wine.'

The comparison was callous, and I didn't think it was deliberately so. Taylor was showing too much empathy, too much of a wish to understand his friend's behaviour.

Justification 101.

Hardly consistent with someone who claimed to feel as betrayed by Moorehead's actions as Taylor.

I said, 'You have a lot of insight into how he felt.'

'I've had a lot of years to think about it.'

'You think he regretted what he did?'

'Killing those boys? Yes ... I mean, I hope so.'

'Really? All these years he never came forward and admitted the truth. Even Ian Brady admitted he had killed people they never found. He just played fast and loose with where they left the remains. But he was strangely proud of what he'd done, I'd say. Alex was always in denial. Not about Justin, but the other boys, the ones that the police linked to him. The ones who were killed when he lived next door.' I took a breath. 'You were with him at least twice when he committed these crimes. And you didn't see anything?'

That got him. Like I'd just slapped a glove across his face and insulted his mother.

'I ... Mr McNee, I didn't like you when we met before. I like you even less now.'

'You're throwing me out?'

He stood up. 'I'm throwing you out.'

I nodded, stood up, too, and said, 'I didn't know better, I'd say you were hiding something.'

'Get out.'

Ernie once warned me that you shouldn't lie to a suspect unless you thought it would get the right reaction.

But I wasn't a copper these days.

What the fuck did it matter?

I tossed it out: 'The mother requested they re-examine the body. He's being dug up as we speak.'

'I want you to leave.'

'Tell me something,' I said. 'Talking about mothers ... you told me you had to see your mother for her birthday? She's been dead thirteen years now. You thought I wouldn't check?'

I didn't see him move. He swung his coffee mug wildly at my head. I was aware of the heat first, as the coffee landed like raindrops on my scalp. Then, as I turned, he caught the side of my face with the mug. It shattered. My head shook, my brain battered around inside my skull. My vision blurred. There was liquid in my eyes, and I realized, only as I went down on my knees that it was more blood than coffee.

I raised my hands, expecting another blow. But it never came.

I fell forward, balanced on my hands to stop from belly-flopping completely. When I realized he was gone, I rolled on to my back, took in deep breaths. After a few moments, I got up, wiped the blood from my vision as best I could. Shaking like an alcoholic in need of his next drink.

'Mr Taylor?'

Was he gone? Waiting for me? Playing games?

The idea didn't fit with what I understood of him. He killed small boys. Defenceless children. To attack a full-grown man was an act of desperation. And if he'd been confident, he would have continued the assault

251

once I went down. I wouldn't have stood a chance. But he didn't know that. In his mind, I was a threat. One he had to run from.

I walked forward a couple of steps, then reached out to balance myself against the back of the white-leather sofa where I'd been sitting a few minutes earlier.

'It doesn't have to be like this,' I said, making sure he could hear me if he was close. 'This can end, now.'

There was still no response.

I pulled out my mobile, dialled Lindsay's number.

'The fuck do you want?'

His boy was in another room, then. 'I'm at Jason Taylor's house.'

'Jason Taylor?'

'The guy who found the evidence against Alex Moorehead. The IT expert Wood called in.'

'Jesus, McNee, leave it alone.'

'I would. Except ... the evidence against Moorehead. Taylor planted it.'

I spoke harshly down the line. All the time looking around, waiting for another attack.

'Jesus, McNee. You really can't leave this shite alone, can you?'

'It was nothing to do with Wood. Call it one of life's little coincidences. Taylor acted on his own.'

'You have proof?' But the question lacked

bite. He already knew what he had to do. I just had to nudge him a little more in the right direction.

'You need to be the one to call it in.'

'Call what in?'

'He killed those boys. That's why Moorehead never copped to it. He was covering for his friend.'

'Fucksakes.'

'You know I wouldn't be calling you if—'

'Fucksakes, I know. I know.'

He hung up.

I was still nauseous. But recovered enough to let go of the sofa. My right leg was numb. I'd had problems with it for years after the accident. Most of the trouble had been psychological; a physical manifestation of my own mental pain. But it still troubled me. Some mornings, I'd wake up, grunting with pain, like the muscles were snapping back on themselves. The sensation would last for a few minutes, but for the rest of the day I'd barely be able to put any weight on my feet.

I limped across the open-plan living area, round to where I saw two doors that led deeper into the house. Maybe the bedroom or the study. 'Taylor! Come on, man. Make this easy on—'

That was when I heard the rumble of rubber on pebble. I half-ran, half-limped to the front door. Saw his car at the end of the drive. He was erratic, turning too wide on to the main road.

I stood where I was.

Watched him disappear.

THIRTY-TWO

I went back inside. Wished I had gloves with me. Could have done a little searching of my own before the cops arrived. As it was, I knew I shouldn't risk contaminating the scene.

But those two doors beckoned to me.

What the hell?

I opened the first, using my sleeve to prevent prints. Found the bedroom. As spotless as the rest of the house. The bed didn't even have the dent of someone having slept there. I could have been walking round a show home.

Why leave me alive?

A fair question. If Taylor had followed through with his attack, he'd have succeeded. The element of surprise. He could have hidden my body, and it would have been a long time before anyone tried to look for me.

Maybe Griggs would have found him eventually. After all, he had some idea of what I was up to. But Taylor didn't know that. From his point of view, it was easier to kill me and dispose of the evidence.

He'd done it before. Years of hiding evidence. Disposing of bodies. Covering his tracks. So why run?

Blind panic?

I saw another door off the bedroom. Walked through. Found what must have been the study. Everything meticulously organized. The bookshelves were mostly textbooks and the self-help manuals I'd imagined. The self-help books were in mint condition. No broken spines. Unread. There for show. Or waiting for another day.

The computer booted fast. Asked me for a password. With the cops on their way, I didn't feel I had the time to try my hand at amateur hacking, so left it alone.

I went back out again. Tried that second door. Expected a bathroom.

Instead I got a short corridor, with two more doors. One of them was locked. The other led where I expected.

I tried the locked door again.

Felt sick. Went outside. Vomited in the grass.

The police showed up fifteen minutes later. Wemyss riding shotgun in the lead car. He came over to me and said, 'What the fuck have you done?'

I was lying on my back. Next to where I'd vomited. Any other day, you might have thought I was catching some rays. But mostly it was that I didn't want to stand up; just wanted to sleep. Exhausted? Concussed? Maybe.

Slowly, I clambered to my feet. Wemyss offered me no help.

'So tell me,' he said. 'What the fuck have you done?'

I gave him the short version. He listened.

Uniforms and techs swarmed the house. I tried to focus on Wemyss. My story came out in short, staccato bursts.

When I was done, he said, 'You didn't leave it alone. Like I asked.'

'I had to know.'

'You didn't call me?'

'Figured you wouldn't like the fact I sneaked evidence out of storage.'

He nodded. 'Care to remind me how you pulled that one off again?'

I shook my head. Some parts of my story, I'd kept deliberately vague. 'I'd get someone in trouble. You know how it is.'

He sneered. 'You should have come to me.'

'Would you have listened?'

'If the evidence was right.'

'All I had was circumstantial.'

'Tell me why he didn't kill you.'

'I don't know.'

There was a yell from the house. One of the uniforms waving his hands. Wemyss made strides towards the front door. I did my best to keep pace. My leg wasn't feeling any better. Kept threatening to just give up, let me topple over.

Inside, the officer explained that they'd broken down the locked door. There was something the DI needed to see.

I followed at a discreet distance, close enough they might mistake me for someone who was meant to be there. Wemyss didn't say a word. Maybe he didn't care.

The door led to a small staircase, and a basement area beneath the main house. The basement was clearly part of the original plan, following those same modern, minimalist lines. But it didn't feel like the kind of feature that Kirsty and Phil would rave about on Channel 4 property programmes. The air was close, and the atmosphere encouraged a reverential silence.

The basement area was dimly lit, like walking into a trendy bar at the point in the evening where most folk would be looking for a quick hook up. There was a second computer system set up here, and glass-fronted bookcases lining the walls. They were filled with photo albums. On the side of the albums were sticky notes with handwritten dates.

I shivered.

Hoped that this wasn't what it looked like.

Wemyss had pulled on rubber gloves – essential equipment for any thinking police detective – and tried to open one of the glass cases.

They were locked.

'Fucksakes,' he said.

He turned on the PC. Another password. Another curse.

Wemyss stomped to the stairs, shouted up for anyone who could 'hack this arsehole's computer!'

Then he came back across to the bookcases, picked up a small lamp that sat on the computer desk and threw it against the glass of one of the bookcases.

He pulled out one of the albums and placed it on the desk.

I stood beside him. 'Was that standard procedure?'

He said, 'You sure you want to be here for this?'

'I was a copper for ten years,' I said. 'I was there when we found what we thought was Alex's original collection.'

'All the same...'

'All the same, I started this and I want to see it through.'

We both knew what we were going to find. But even when you expect it, there's nothing can stop that unnerving sensation skittering up your spine, making your stomach steel itself against an onslaught of nausea.

Both Wemyss and I had seen people at their worst; the strange and terrible things they can do in the name of their own desires.

But it didn't stop you from fooling yourself into thinking that these things were aberrations, that once you had seen them, you would never come across them again.

People have a habit of constantly disappointing.

Wemyss opened the album.

The label said, 'March 1995 – Oct 1995'.

Inside, we found snaps of children. Mostly boys. Aged between around eight and thirteen. None of the images were particularly damning in and of themselves. The kids were fully clothed, happy, healthy.

But every image had been taken from a distance. They were the kind of candid shots that you learn about from social workers and the detectives who've worked the paedophile circuit.

The people who take these pictures, they store the images, fetishize, fantasize.

It's early stage stuff or else it's like an appetizer before dinner.

The idea is enough to put me off my food. Enough to make me want to beat the fuck out of someone.

I'm no stranger to violence. I've hurt people. They all deserved it to one degree or another, but my anger with them had always been overly personal and occasionally even misdirected.

Now, it felt justified. Pure and simple. The rage was not for myself or my own loss or my own pain. It was for others. Those too weak to defend themselves, too young to suffer the kind of indignity and betrayal that this monster had inflicted upon them.

Not just the dead.

But also those in the albums. The ones he had never touched but had thought about enough that he catalogued and categorized them. As though they were objects, possessions, things to be desired.

'Think he was looking for a career as a photographer?' Wemyss asked, shooting for a black humour to avoid the discomfort and the horror of what we were uncovering. But it couldn't be sidestepped for long.

When I'd talked to Taylor earlier, and we'd both pretended I was still talking about Moorehead, he'd been desperate to rationalize and excuse the monstrous actions of a child-killer, to explain the motivation. Making like it was some kind of sickness of the mind. Something that might even be deserving of sympathy from those who couldn't share his urges.

I'd known, then. I'd have been an idiot not to see it.

But all the same I hadn't wanted to understand what he was trying to tell me. There was part of me wanted to be mistaken. Because that kind of truth is something most people can't comprehend, don't want to face.

Because when you do, you finally realize the depths of horror that humanity is capable of. And you have to wonder why we even deserve to go on living.

Taylor had known that I suspected the truth. We had spoken around the subject because I couldn't confront him. But he wanted me to know that he wasn't the evil monster I would think him to be.

That was why he'd run. Because even he knew the truth.

That he was a monster. That even though he'd tried, he could never succeed in passing on the guilt of his crimes to another man.

That guilt consumed him, as it did so many of these monsters. Yet he couldn't bring himself to stop, or even admit what it was that he did.

Wemyss said, 'Care to take a guess why Moorehead lied for this bawbag?'

I shook my head.

How could I figure it out?

Maybe it was because they were friends. Maybe because he couldn't stand the idea of his friend being responsible for such acts and convinced himself that somehow he was doing the right thing in coming forward because, in the end, someone always has to pay. Or maybe there was something deeper, darker, more sinister than either Wemyss or I could imagine.

Maybe there was no simple explanation.

Just a tangled mess of the worst that humanity has to offer.

Only two men had any of the answers. One of them took his own life. And the other was last seen driving his car to God knows where. He could still be driving. He could have gone to ground. Hell, he could even be trying to kill himself, realizing there was no other way out.

Part of me hoped he was dead. That he took the same way out as Moorehead. That he finally understood the depths of what he had done.

But then the cool, rational part of my brain wanted to get him alone in a room. Not to beat the ever-living shite out of him or to punish him in any way, but to find the truth behind the disappeared, the dead and the destroyed. To make sense of all the horror that he had brought into the world. And then, once I'd done that, I'd let the other part of me strangle the fucker with my bare hands.

The tech at the computer said, 'We're in.'

Wemyss turned away from the album. 'What have we got?'

'I'll need to take the machine and have a proper look. Lots of encrypted files. Mostly media. Video, audio, images...'

I was lightheaded.

'I need some fucking air.'

I made my way out of the basement, towards the world above, craving the cleansing breath of the wind and the sting of the salt carried from the nearby sea that might help me to feel part of the human race once again.

THIRTY-THREE

We met at her dad's old place. Over a year and a half after his death, it was still on the market. They'd done it up inside and out, but with the recession and the economy, it was proving difficult to shift. In a strange way, I didn't want it to sell. The house was all that was left of Ernie. While it was still unoccupied, it felt as though you could walk past one day and find he had returned.

Susan met me on the drive. Looking up at the house as though trying to figure out whether there was still some part of her dad left inside somewhere.

I said, 'How long have you known?'

'He didn't tell me, if that's what you mean,' she said. 'He might have admitted it, eventually. But you know how he was. Liked to keep everything close. Didn't ask for help unless he needed it. When I was a girl, Mum used to steal his keys and lock him in if she thought he was too unwell to go to work. She'd call ahead and let them know, but she knew that unless he lost both his legs, he'd still try and walk into FHQ, as if he could carry the world on his shoulders.'

'He was police through and through,' I said.

She smiled. 'Mum and me got lucky, though. It was never at the expense of family.'

She was wearing rose-tints, of course. Her parents had divorced a few years before Ernie's death. In part, due to the secrecy that Ernie had shrouded himself in for the past few years. Yes, he'd always been a family man as much as a policeman, but the nature of his covert work for Griggs and his predecessors had finally taken its toll. Ernie never told his wife the truth. How could he?

'Does your mum know? That you're back?'

Susan shook her head. Walked to the front door, unlocked it. Ushered me inside.

The hall was dark. Dust motes floated in the air, caught in the light that came from outside.

Everything was still.

We were intruders.

I followed Susan to the kitchen. They hadn't yet cleared out Ernie's utensils. Pots, pans, even a kettle. The house didn't appear as empty as I expected and it took me a few moments to realize why. 'You've been living here?'

Susan nodded as she switched the kettle on. 'Just temporary,' she said. 'While we're in the city.'

The casualness of the 'we' caught me, but then, maybe I was paranoid. After everything that had happened over the last few weeks, I had every right to be suspicious of anything anyone told me.

Maybe I needed to book time in with a masseuse. Try and work out the tension. Relax a little. The next few months were going to be about deception.

Months?

Ernie had been working Burns for years as far as I could tell. What had it got him?

Dead.

What was it going to do to me?

'Here,' Susan said, and handed me a black coffee. She had a mug of her own, but the whole time we talked, she didn't take even a sip.

'You wanted to talk.'

'Aye,' I said. 'You were gone for...'

'I was abroad five months,' she said. 'Went through Europe, saw all the sights you want to see. Decided that Prague might have been beautiful once. Before it became the number-one destination for stag parties. Realized that you can lose yourself in Rome or Paris in the same way you can become lost in a dream and never want to wake up. I even got a little baked in Amsterdam.' She smiled. But only with her lips. 'Then I went east. Did all the backpacking tours. Seemed like a good idea. I'd never done the whole gap-year thing. Seemed like a plan, a good way to rediscover myself.'

'Did you meet any mystics?'

'No,' she said. 'It still seemed like bullshit to me. Guess Daddy really did raise a practical girl.' She put her mug down on the worktop. 'I missed you, Steed. I really did. Every day. Some mornings I'd wake up, wonder why I'd left you behind.'

'So why did you?'

She chewed at her lower lip. Her brow furrowed, gently, and her eyes looked down as though she could find the answers in her coffee. 'You know why. I meant what I said when I left. Everything between us was complicated. Too many secrets.'

I understood, I really did.

'When did you find out the truth?'

'It was Griggs who got in touch with me. He's persistent. Guess you know that. Emails. Phone messages. The whole treatment. He didn't come out and say it, not until I got back, but he told me that what he had to talk about was to do with Dad. That I couldn't share it with anyone.'

'I used to work with Griggs.'

'He remembers you. Not like you are now. You were uniform then. Says you always had a spark, but that you seemed too in awe of authority to really come out of your shell.'

'I was learning. Besides, he's one to talk about people changing.'

We moved through to the living room. Nothing had changed. Even though she must have been here for at least a month, there was no sign of occupation. The furniture was the same. The bookshelves, even the DVD collection were still Ernie's.

As I sat down in an armchair, I became aware of the stillness around us. Like the house was holding its breath.

Maybe Ernie really was still here, somewhere, watching us. I wondered what he'd think, whether he'd approve of what happened between me and Susan.

If things had been different, I like to think he would have. If things hadn't turned sour between all three of us, I like to think that he would have given us his blessing.

And that he might have tried to intervene when things went wrong.

'What was he like, then? The man you remember?'

'Griggs? Passionate. Idealistic. Angry, too. Had a thing for wife-beaters.'

'Still does. One of the reasons he came to SCDEA, he could do the work without getting personally involved.'

'You don't think he's personally involved? He wants to lay out Burns as much as anyone I've ever met.'

'Even my dad?'

'Your dad must have known that no matter what he did trying to take down Burns the way he did, it would be the end of his life on both sides. He couldn't turn because he'd be a traitor to Burns, and he couldn't stay a cop because there would be people who would never understand what he'd done, who would think of him as a bent copper looking for any way to save his skin.'

'Which is why I suggested you.'

For just a moment, I didn't know how to respond. I just looked at her, and got a blank in my brain, as though some switch had been tripped and I was lost between sensations.

'You can walk the line,' Susan said. 'You're not a cop. You're not a criminal.'

'But I need my clients to trust me,' I said.

'The ABI,' she said. 'We can make that go away. We can...'

'Sure,' I said. 'On paper. I think I know why your dad did it. He was close to retiring. It didn't matter to him. He could go out in a blaze of glory. And I'm sure there was a handsome payout involved, too. One that could set you up if anything were to happen to him.'

'I never received any money. Neither did Mum.'

'Maybe you should ask Griggs,' I said. Then I stopped myself. The old anger was coming through. The stubborn, obstinate anger that had stopped me from being a fully functioning member of the human race for so long. I let it die. Said, 'I'm sorry. It's just that what I'm about to do ... Just tell me, Susan, do you think things might have worked out different for us? I mean, if Ernie was still alive? If he was the one telling us the truth about what he was doing with Burns?'

She leaned in and kissed me gently on the cheek.

When she pulled back, there was a moment's silence. Strained. Uncomfortable. The way it had been before she left; an unanswered question still between us.

I said, 'You never told me.'

'Should I have to?'

When we discovered that Kevin Wood was in part responsible for her father's death, Susan had snapped, kidnapped the deputy chief constable and locked him in a storage unit. Her actions were never made public. She had avoided the glare of the officers investigating Wood's actions.

Which would have been fine for me if not for one loose end.

Kevin Wood never went to trial. The investigation into his actions was conducted posthumously. He had been found in the storage locker, burned alive following what arson investigators ruled a freak accident.

When I left Wood in the locker, he was alive.

I always had my doubts as to how the fire had started.

Susan knew it. Refused to answer my

questions.

There were too many secrets between us, me and Susan. Too many doubts and uncertainties. No wonder we'd been a bad match.

No wonder she'd left.

I said, 'No. You shouldn't.'

'You're always looking for secrets, Steed,' she said. 'All the time. Even when there aren't any.'

'Yeah?'

She shook her head. But she smiled.

I decided that was enough of an answer for me.

THIRTY-FOUR

'You have a ... David Burns is here to see you.'

Dot was pretty good at keeping a neutral air around most clients, but David Burns had this way of getting to people. Maybe it was the sanctimonious air of hypocrisy that hung around him. Didn't need a caged canary to catch a whiff of that.

He came through, smiling, offering his free hand. 'Always said you were like a dog with a bone, son.' I couldn't help but notice the envelope he had with him. What was he carrying? A reward?

I nodded. This wasn't how I'd intended to approach Burns. The idea had been to wait for Taylor to be arrested, for the whole damn thing to be over. But with Taylor on the run, and currently nowhere to be found, it was only a matter of time before word reached the old man.

No doubt he had someone on the inside. His kind always do.

He sat down without being asked. I swallowed my pride, let it pass without comment. 'I don't like to see the guilty go un-punished.'

'Something we have in common,' he said. 'A crime like that is ... unforgiveable.'

'There are victims that are off limits,' I said.

He smiled. 'We talk around things all the time, you and me,' he said. 'Never quite saying what we really mean. I think that's what gives rise to ... misunderstandings between us. I'm no angel, I accept that. I've had to. People in my life, they have to make choices that privileged people can't always understand.'

'And here was me thinking you wanted to be friends.'

'You always had some learning to do about life. I think leaving the police was the best thing you ever did, son.'

'Yeah?'

'You know I've always had an interest in you. Because I think you've been learning more and more about how to make hard choices. My overtures have been a bit ... enthusiastic, I admit. But I see potential in you.'

I felt the familiar clench. The knot in my stomach and the tremors in my hands that told me the only way to relieve the tension was to bodily chuck the old fucker out of the office. Preferably through the window.

While it was still closed.

But I held the urge in check. Wondering if he noticed.

'It's getting hard to tell who the bad guys are any more.'

'You sound like him, you know.'

'Who?'

'Ernie.'

'Bright?'

He nodded. 'I told you before,' he said. 'We were old friends.'

'He tried to take you down more than once.'

'He was a copper. That was his job. But I think he always understood the need for men like me.'

I nodded. 'You went to school together, didn't you?'

He nodded. Around a year and a half earlier, he'd given me a potted history of their friendship in an attempt to explain why Ernie had appeared – to me at least – to be a crooked copper, not the hero I'd always thought he was.

Three years ago, before Ernie's murder, I'd discovered this apparent friendship, while working a case that had deep ties to Burns. The old man had been throwing a party at his house when I went round to talk to him about a case that had been troubling me. I wound up threatening Burns, shoving him against the wall. Then one of his guests inter-vened. The shock of that guest being Ernie

Bright, the man who had embodied every-thing that being a detective ever meant to me, quelled my anger, turned it into a be-trayed confusion.

Ernie died before we could ever really talk about what had happened that night.

But something in my brain was beginning to click. Connections that had been dispar-ate before now started to come together. Back in the nineties, Ernie had been Burns's contact on the force during a brief period when the police had taken it into their heads to work unofficially with the devils they knew to take down the devils they didn't. According to Burns, that partnership had outlasted the operation because of the two men's shared background. But there was something else going on, something that I hadn't been aware of.

That even Burns wasn't aware of.

Something that tied together all the ap-parent contradictions surrounding Ernie Bright.

I said, 'In the grand scheme of things, you keep a tidy house. Your operations are run like a business.'

He smiled. 'This isn't really the place to talk about such things.'

I relented. Too eager. He wanted to trust me because of whatever bond he felt was between us. But he hadn't got where he was today by being an idiot. Like Taylor, he understood the need to hide in public the things he did in private. But oddly, I was beginning to understand his long-standing argument about the relativism of criminal activity, and how he was less of a monster than someone like Taylor.

But that didn't make him less of a criminal. Not to me, and certainly it wouldn't have to Ernie. No, even if they had been friends, I knew that Ernie was not the kind of man to confuse his principles in the way Burns had described.

Why was Susan working with SCDEA on this project?

Why was she so desperate for me to get in close with Burns?

It made sense. Absolute sense. When you stopped to think about it.

I said, 'Maybe we can talk about things later. I can tell you what I know about Taylor.'

He stood up. 'If you hear anything about this pervert, where he is, whatever, give me a call. I'd like to see him face justice.'

'You mean you want to be the one to call in the cops?'

He found that funny enough to give me a chuckle. 'Something like that. I guess we'll see,' he said. 'In the meantime I have a proposition for you. Things have changed between us. I'm sure of that. We have an understanding.'

I shrugged.

He put the envelope on the table. Patted it. 'Maybe I'm wrong. But I think we might do when you see this. When you hear my little proposition.'

I looked at the envelope. A sick feeling built in my stomach.

'Five years,' the old bugger says. 'Five years since I offered you the chance to come and work with me...'

THIRTY-FIVE

Do you like taking photographs?

The kind of grubby work that gave the investigative gig a bad name. The equivalent of scouting for cheating spouses or, worse, hacking phones for desperate showbiz journos.

And yet this was the test he gave me.

Clever, when you thought about it. Had the dual effect of testing my loyalty and alienating me from potential allies on the other side.

What I wanted to do was throw the assignment in his face, and him out the door. But instead, I walked out calmly, with the assignment in hand and the stain on my soul.

I was in.

At least, I had my foot in the door. Now I just had to make sure I could squeeze my whole body through what gap there was.

Getting the images he wanted was easy enough. All I had to do was book a room for the night at the Apex. I told the guy on the desk that a friend had stayed before, really liked this room on the top floor, and if there was any way he could give me the same one, I'd be grateful. A simple lie. Worked easy enough, too.

The room was good. Inside, I set myself up for the evening, figured I might have to wait a night or two to get what I wanted. What Burns wanted.

I set up the camera via the air conditioning, snaking the endoscope camera through the pipes, feeding it slowly until I came up against the grille on the other side.

The other end was connected via USB to a laptop. I positioned the machine where I could see what was happening, then turned on the TV and settled in for the night.

They came in at around 10 p.m.

I noticed the movement, got up, watched the images on the laptop. The frame rate was a little jerky, but it did the job. They kept the lights on low, but it was enough. I didn't have to adjust for night vision.

They moved with the slightly awkward gait that came with a little too much wine for dinner. I was glad there was no sound. I didn't want to hear what she had to say to him just before she kissed him.

The camera recorded everything.

At a certain point, I figured I had enough to satisfy Burns, stopped the camera taking images.

There was a dead weight in my stomach. I knew what Burns really wanted. There was a very good reason he had handed me this assignment. And you don't want to upset the client by failing to give them what they really want.

I started the camera again.

They were done. Finished. Lying in bed together. If either of them smoked, they'd probably have sparked up.

Or not.

The room was, after all, non-smoking.

I left my room, went next door, hammered hard enough to wake the dead. Took about thirty seconds before Griggs answered. He was wearing the complimentary hotel dressing gown. His features crinkled with an unasked question.

I punched him in the face. He fell back. I walked inside.

Susan was out of bed, on her feet. 'Steed!'

I shook my head, grabbed Griggs by the shoulders and pushed him against a wall. 'There's a camera in the duct. Recording all of this. No sound. But it sees everything that's going on.'

'What the fuck?'

'You wanted me to get on Burns's good side, this goes a long way.'

'Do it, then, you prick!'

I punched him in the stomach. He doubled.

Susan grabbed my shoulder, spun me round. 'I'm sorry I didn't tell you ... I

281

didn't...'

'It's fine,' I said. I lifted my hands. I would only take this so far, and it would stretch credulity for me to attack Susan as well. 'It's fine.'

I backed off.

Susan looked ready to say something.

Griggs slowly started to straighten. Coughing hard.

I went back to my room, pulled the camera roughly back through. Killed the feed.

'Fuck you,' I said, as though Burns was in the room with me.

And sent him the file.

THIRTY-SIX

I spent most of the next day killing time. A package arrived with a disposable mobile enclosed. A note from Griggs attached. The note detailed drop points and contacts. The mobile was only for use in emergency situations.

After Dot was done for the day, I hung around, checking and double-checking old emails. Flipping case files. Feeling nauseous. Thinking about what I was about to do.

I had to be certain. Know that this was the right thing.

Getting close to Burns as Griggs wanted would mean abandoning every principle I'd ever had. It wasn't just about adjusting my behaviour for a few minutes or hours, it was about losing myself to a life I detested.

I had to be sure.

Griggs's initial approach had been to intimidate me with Kellen's threat of investigation and incarceration. When that hadn't worked, he'd tried to seduce me, using Susan. And again when that didn't work, he'd appealed to my sense of morality, such as it was.

Everyone has their own unique moral compass. There are lines that some people won't cross, which others wouldn't even consider an issue. We all answer to ourselves in the end. No God. No eternity of damnation. Just our own conscience.

All I wanted was for the guilty to be punished, the innocent to be protected. Or, if it came to it, avenged. The means to that end used to be important to me. But principles can only take you so far. It's the intention that counts.

Right?

Maybe Burns and I weren't so different after all.

When we were at her father's house, two days earlier, I'd asked Susan why she hadn't approached Burns, why Griggs hasn't asked her to be the one to get close. After all, she'd have been perfect. She'd be able to finish her father's work, and all that anger over his death would play perfectly into why she would be looking to work with a man like Burns.

'I couldn't do it,' she told me. 'Last year, I did things that ... I hated myself, Steed, for what I did. I left one man to die, tried to kill another in cold blood. All because I was angry. Needed to hurt someone like I'd been hurt myself.'

I listened to her confession. We both knew

that I understood. Because I had done the things that she had stopped herself from doing. Because I had crossed the lines that she could never bring herself to step over.

I closed down the PC, went to the window and looked out to the street. Across the way, the Benefits Office was closed, but a couple of old jakeys were hanging round near the disabled ramp sharing a bottle out of a bag and laughing at something only they would ever see the humour in.

The skies were clouding over. Night was stealing across the city.

Night time was when I'd always felt at my most comfortable. The daylight hours were an obligation; a concession to the majority. I'd work them if I had to, but when the sun went down, I was at my most awake. When I was young, my parents had told me I was a night owl, that I'd be best getting a job as a nightwatchman. They weren't far wrong.

Griggs had this strange idea that all I needed to do was break a few laws to prove that I was on the old man's side. My confrontation with him at the hotel would show that any trust we might have had in each other was broken, and more importantly so was my relationship with Susan. But Burns wasn't daft. No matter what I did, he'd smell a rat. He wouldn't trust me without good reason, and if my descent seemed too fast and convenient, he'd know something was wrong.

He would test me again. But not in the way that Griggs might expect. Burns wouldn't ask me to take point on an armed robbery or beat up some poor schmuck who got behind on payments. He was too smart for that. He would test me in other ways, without me even knowing what he was doing. Burns liked to think of himself as a master manipulator, as a man who understood the human condition. All self-taught, of course. He was working class made good. He was what he believed other people aspired to. Had pulled himself up to a position of power through hard work and sheer determination. And all the way, he'd tell you, he took care of his own. Because in this world, that's what you have to do.

He believed it, too. There was no acting with Burns when it came to his own motivations. He genuinely believed that he was working for some greater good, that all the things he did were out of necessity, that he was some flawed hero in his own bloody story.

He wanted people like me to realize that about him. Why he kept insisting that we were somehow the same. He was looking for vindication. God knows why he chose me, but he did. That was what made me the ideal person to become Griggs's stooge. More than Susan, maybe even more than Ernie.

But like I said, the old man wasn't stupid.

He'd expect me to fight what was happening, at least for a while.

And he'd expect me to sacrifice something for the greater good, as he saw it. One of my principles, perhaps. He'd dress it up like his way was the only truly moral choice.

I started to close up, shutting down the computer, checking that nothing was left on that didn't need to be.

Figured a beer might help me make sense of things.

When I went out into reception, I heard someone knocking at the door.

'We're closed,' I shouted. 'For the evening.'

They insisted. Rattling at the door, then battering it with their fists. Like they couldn't figure out why we weren't open at their beck and call.

I sighed, went to the door and opened it. 'If you call back tomorrow, you can make an appoint—'

I stepped back.

Taylor rammed the door open with his shoulder, pushing against my weight. He had the element of surprise, knocked me off balance.

I stumbled a few steps, knocked against Dot's desk, managed to right myself.

That was when I saw him come at me with the hammer.

THIRTY-SEVEN

I twisted back, felt the hammer rush past where my face had been a second earlier. Which was good, meant that he was off balance. I let my momentum carry me, taking the weight on my hands, balancing on the desk, and raising one leg swiftly. Caught Taylor a good one in the balls.

He didn't drop the hammer, but he stepped back, posture crumpling, instinct making him try to protect himself. I took the opportunity to increase the distance between us, moving behind the desk, trying to regain some semblance of control.

This wasn't the first time someone had tried to kill me in my own office. Five years back, I'd watched my then secretary shot in the stomach by two psychos who had threatened my life moments earlier.

Maybe it was the building.

Or just these offices.

Taylor straightened up, his features crooked. This was the man as he really was: a monster. A machine of violence and hate and ugliness.

He was wearing the same clothes I'd seen him in three days earlier. He hadn't shaved. Hadn't slept either.

He was ready to kill me. I still wondered why he hadn't before.

'Think you can do it?'

He hesitated, still holding the hammer, body a bear-trap of tension. 'Do what?'

'Kill me.'

'I've killed. You know I have.'

'Right,' I said. 'Little boys. Kids too innocent to defend themselves. Big fucking killer that you are.' Sure, taunt the man with the hammer.

He was breathing hard. Barely able to keep control over his own body. Kept licking at his lips, then swallowing.

'You got lucky,' I said. 'Before. Element of surprise. So put down the hammer, and we'll see how this plays out in a fair fight.'

He shook his head. 'Mr Fucking Hero, eh? What do you know?'

'I know that you've lived with all this for way too long. You tried to tell me the other day how it was a sickness, a compulsion.'

'No, I...'

'I think you tried to tell me something else, too. Your mother. When I mentioned her...'

'Don't. Just don't.'

'Did she hurt you?'

'You don't fucking understand.'

'And your father?'

289

He swallowed hard. His breathing got heavy, catching in his chest. The long hair had started to matt against his face, caught in the sweat that poured out of him.

'Did they know what kind of monster you were? Your first kill came after your mother's death.'

'Shut up!'

'You can get help, Taylor.'

'Too late for that. Too many...'

'How many?'

He dropped his head for a moment. I could still see his eyes. They were moving from side to side in a strange kind of way. His lips were moving, too. And I realized: *He was counting.*

I remembered the dream. All those faces staring back at me from the walls. The presence outside the room that I could sense coming closer with each tick of my watch.

I had felt terrified, then. Adrenaline pumping.

Fear was close to answer.

Do we ever escape who we are?

Taylor had never been able to escape his own sickening compulsions. No matter how hard he tried to become a respectable man, what he had done was always there. Even if he told himself that he would never act on those urges again, the possibility was still within him that one day he would. He could change his behaviour, but who he was inside would never really change.

In that sense, we were the same.

We both tried to deny who we were, but could never escape the truth.

He was a monster. I was driven by rage.

At the monsters of this world. The ones who hurt others for no reason other than they can.

He was still counting his victims when I rushed him. He tried to swing with the hammer, but it was too late. I grabbed his wrist, swung him in a strange parody of a waltz and slammed that arm down against Dot's desk. He caught the edge of the wooden top with the back of his wrist. His fingers spasmed, let go of the hammer.

I followed up fast, slamming my forehead against the soft bridge of his nose. He cried out and went limp. I pulled back, let him slump to the floor. The hammer was still within his reach. I kicked it away and stood over him. My breath came heavy, my chest tight with exertion.

'Not so tough when they fight back, are you?'

He didn't say anything.

'You ever been in a real fight?'

He looked up at me. His nose was broken. Blood soaked his upper lip and down his chin. He spat and said, 'Cunt.'

'Get up,' I said.

He climbed to his feet. He was unsteady.

'Sit down.'

He did so, taking Dot's chair. Glared at me. Didn't bother trying to wipe the blood away from his nose. Right now he probably didn't feel it so bad. He'd be running on the post-adrenaline spike. The pain would settle in later when he had time to process what had happened. Right now he was humiliated more than anything.

It was about to get much worse.

'This what they did to you? What you wanted to do to those kids? Make them hurt like you did?'

'You'll never understand.'

I picked up the phone.

'Calling the police?' His voice sounded stuffed up. Like he had a bad cold. Between words he snorted, clearing his airways as the blood gathered.

I ignored him, finished dialling, listened to the tones on the other end of the line. Finally, a man answered. I didn't recognize him. All I said was, 'Tell him it's McNee. Tell him I have a gift.'

When I hung up, I looked over at Taylor.

He didn't look so cocky any more.

He looked like a man who'd just realized his nightmare was real.

The big man didn't come himself. I hadn't expected him to make a personal appearance, of course. He didn't take risks. That was how he'd evaded arrest for so long.

The two men who came to the office were burly, dressed like bouncers, looking like they'd rather be in shellsuits and trainers. But Burns was a businessman through and through, preferring his associates try to dress properly. Intimidation through professionalism.

'Who're these guys?' Taylor asked. His plummy tones had vanished. His voice had taken on a rougher accent, betraying his roots.

I didn't say anything.

Neither did the two thugs. They hauled him to his feet.

'I thought you were going to call the cops!' Taylor said. 'I thought you were calling the fucking cops!'

My mobile buzzed from the desk.

A text message.

Number withheld.

An address.

Nothing more.

I watched as the thugs frogmarched Taylor out the front door. He was protesting the whole way, wriggling like a fish caught on a hook. His protests were shaky, terrified. He had expected the comforting arms of the cops. Instead, he was being taken somewhere by two men who looked like they could crush his head with one hand.

He was frightened.

Good.

I waited until he was out of earshot, down the stairs. Then I went to the bathroom and vomited into the bowl.

When I was done, I sat down on the floor and slowed my breathing. My muscles ached.

There was no turning back, now.

THIRTY-EIGHT

The Murder House.

That's what we used to call it.

On the outskirts of the city, a crumbling Victorian presence, with overgrown gardens and decaying facade. I've never seen it for sale, never been sure who owned it. It was one of those buildings that didn't really change, that people knew existed but never paid attention to.

Perhaps because of its history.

Some buildings become their history. They become entwined with a particular narrative and the more years pass, the more that narrative takes hold of the building, becomes part of its very structure.

That was the Murder House.

I dare you to knock on the door.

I dare you to look in the window.

I dare you to go inside.

We were kids. The idea of a house haunted by a gruesome murder was irresistible. But none of us knew the real truth. All we had were half-heard and half-remembered whispers.

I wouldn't discover the truth until years later when I joined the force.

The Murder House had belonged to a man named Charles Leigh. He was a family man, 2.4 kids, a good mid-level management job, the whole dream. He'd never been in trouble with the police, never shown any signs of instability. He was what you'd call a model citizen. But the trouble with normal, as a man like Jason Taylor proved, is that it's too often a mask for real troubles.

Leigh was the kind of man who lived beyond his means, and in the 1980s, when the recession hit, found himself facing a world of troubles he'd never anticipated. But he could never admit to any problems, and continued to live the same lifestyle with mounting bills that he kept hidden from his wife and kids.

What happened next is a little unclear. Leigh started killing people for money. He didn't take contracts or work for any local gangsters. What he did was break into old people's houses, kill them, and take whatever valuables he could find. He killed three pensioners before the police finally caught up to him.

Leigh was a keen amateur shooter, regularly took part in shoots on estates outside the city. He kept three shotguns in the home, all legally obtained and licensed. He was careful and fastidious about safety. He kept them locked away, where the kids couldn't get at them. Ammunition was stored in a separate room. He respected the weapons, understood what they were capable of.

And then the police came to his door.

Leigh knew why they were there. He knew that they'd worked out his scheme. And he panicked. He took his wife and younger daughter hostage. Locked them in the house with him. Threatened them with one of his shotguns. Didn't make demands. Just kept the police at bay, maybe hoping against hope that there was a way out.

But there wasn't.

Charles Leigh was an inept killer. He wasn't cut out to be a murderer.

He had only done what he did out of desperation, the pressures of maintaining his expected lifestyle in the midst of a recession finally proving too much for him.

The standoff took place over eight hours. The police thought they'd finally talked Leigh down from his desperation. They were ready to enter the house when Leigh killed his wife. His daughter.

And finally, as the police rushed into the bedroom where he had been holed up, Leigh killed himself. They thought that he had tried to employ the shotgun in his mouth, but the length of the barrel would have given him difficulty, so they walked in on him as he slit his own throat. That was the worst thing, according to the officers who witnessed it. Slitting your own throat takes an amount of desperation and will. It's tricky and messy. Most folk can't do it. But Leigh had snapped in the final moments of the siege. Maybe he knew it would be worse for him to be taken in alive. He died two minutes later. Drowned in his own blood.

The Murder House.

No one lived there after that. Even over two decades later, it remained empty, a strange and abandoned shell at the end of a long street of similar houses.

This was the address that had arrived at my mobile.

I saw the van across the street. White, nondescript, same plates as the one that had pulled up outside my offices thirty minutes earlier.

I looked at the Murder House. Remembered my childhood fears. I'd never been brave enough to go inside. The idea of the poor tormented souls of a dead family haunting the place had been enough to give me nightmares.

Now, I had no choice but to enter.

I walked up the broken and chipped garden path. Beyond crazy paving, now, it was overgrown with weeds and overhanging branches from the neglected bushes that had once gently marked its boundaries.

I paused at the front door.

The old fear gathering inside. That sick-to-the-stomach feeling that comes with irrational panic.

Pushing down the sensation, I opened the door. Walked inside.

'Glad you finally made it.'

They were in the large dining room at the rear of the ground floor. The space was empty, except for one chair in the very centre. Taylor was tied to the chair with plastic ties. Naked. Bloodier than when I last saw him. And very still. Not slumped. Not dead. Just still.

Expectant.

Floodlights illuminated him. A generator hummed.

Burns and his thugs stood just outside the circles of light. Watching this pathetic, naked man as he sat there bathed in harsh light, waiting for something to happen.

'What are you going to do to him?' I asked.

'Little late in asking,' Burns said. 'Nah, we're just going to have a wee chat, me and Mr Taylor here. That's all. A natter. A friendly discussion.' His voice sounded tight. I realized I'd never seen him like this. I'd known him simply as a manipulator, as a puppet-master. He had always been the man directing the action, never participating. This evening, he was ready to step up to the plate, remind people why he was feared.

I'd seen pictures of Burns in his younger days. A full head of black hair swept back from the temples. Piercing eyes that remained with him even in old age. A slash of cruelty across his features, so that even when he was smiling, he looked ready to lash out at anyone who dared disagree with him.

Old age changes what we can do, makes us rethink how best to achieve our goals. But it doesn't change who we are.

At his core, Burns was a maelstrom of violence. He had developed a veneer of civility, but strip that away and you saw the raw, animal instincts beneath.

I felt a rush of adrenaline. An urge to grab Taylor, haul him out of this hell and dump him in a cell. Looking at him, exposed under the harsh lights, I saw a pathetic shell of a man who was suddenly confronted with the horror of his own life, who realized the price of all the bad things he had ever done.

Wasn't this punishment enough?

What had I thought would happen when I gave him to Burns?

I knew that he would be hurt. But I had thought that it was a price worth paying to get closer to the old man. Now, all I wanted to do was run away from what I had done.

Griggs was asking me to become what Burns wanted me to be. Asking me to go deep into the world of a vicious sociopath and refuse to blink at the horrors I saw there.

He was asking me to become complicit in order to bring an end to the violence and terror that swirled around this man.

Could I do that?

I had honestly believed that I could. And maybe even just six months earlier, it might have been possible. But I had started to re-join the human race again, to gain a measure of empathy that had been missing for so long.

Now, the idea of stepping into the shadows with men like Burns repulsed me. I knew what he was going to do here, tonight. And I wasn't sure any more that I could simply stand by and let it happen.

In the back of my mind, a voice urged that men like Taylor deserved the very worst that happened to them. But could I bring myself to follow through on that voice? It went against everything I believed in.

I killed a man once.

He deserved it.

I don't know how long we stood there, the four of us, watching the naked man under the harsh lights. None of us said a word. Neither did Taylor.

Finally, Burns stepped into the light.

He grabbed a folding chair, and sat in front of Taylor. The two men looked at each other. Neither looking away. Taylor's fear had turn-ed into a kind of defiance. He knew what was going to happen. He wasn't going to give up crying and screaming and blubbing. There was an odd dignity in that.

A dignity I knew that David Burns would rip down.

It would be a mercy to kill him now. Slit his throat. Let him bleed out.

But, the little voice in my head whispered, a monster like that doesn't deserve mercy.

THIRTY-NINE

'Do you know who I am?'

Taylor spat blood on the floor.

Burns said, 'I'm a father. I'm a concerned citizen.'

'You're going to kill me.'

Burns shook his head. 'Why would I do that?'

'Were any of them yours?'

'The children? No. None of them. But I knew a little boy. Davey Simpson.'

'Davey,' said Taylor. Then he smiled. 'I remember Davey. He liked trains.'

'Yes, he liked trains.'

'How did you know Davey?'

'He and his mum lived near me for a while. It was a tragedy when he disappeared.'

'Yes.'

'I tried to kill Alex Moorehead. Do you know that? I arranged for your friend to die.'

'You fucked up.'

'Aye, I did that. I fucked up. Glad I did, now. I'm a direct man, Mr Taylor. I treat people the way they deserve to be treated. If I had killed an innocent man, it would weigh on my conscience.'

Any other time, I might have laughed. The sanctimonious shite flowed easily from the old man. He was a master at self-deception. He actually believed all of this. He saw himself as the one good man left in the world. All his actions came from the best of intentions. He was merely acting the way the world made him act.

It was the only way he could live with the things he did.

In the same way that Taylor denied his most basic instincts, denied the sickness in his mind.

The two of them had more in common than they might have guessed.

Burns sat back in the chair. Relaxed. I thought that if things had been different, he'd have been an asset in any interview. He'd have made a good cop.

Then again, sometimes there's a thin line between those who uphold the law and those who break it.

'I don't understand,' he said. 'Why you would kill a boy like Davey.'

'Understand?'

'He was a sweet fucking child, Mr Taylor. He was curious about the world. He loved his mother. He wanted to drive trains when he grew up. And you killed him.'

'I...'

Burns leaned forward.

'I...'

Burns reached up and grabbed Taylor's chin, pulling the man's face around so he couldn't look away.

'Tell me.'

'I ... he ... I didn't mean to kill him. I didn't mean to kill any of them.'

'But you did.'

'Yes.'

'Why?'

'It was an accident.'

'And those other boys?'

'I never meant to ... they're ... I look at them, I want to be their friend and then...'

'Tell me.' Burns was soft. Gentle. Sickeningly empathetic. I wanted to walk over there and beat the living shite out of the pathetic specimen of humanity tied to the chair. But Burns – the master of sudden and brutal violence – was taking his time, treating the fuck with kid gloves, letting him slowly divulge his secrets.

How could he do this? How could he suppress his own instincts?

When I came in, what I saw was a man with murder in his eyes. And now here he was, keeping all of that rage buried inside and talking oh-so-gently, the way he might have done with a child.

'It's a sickness,' Taylor said. 'I know I have a problem. I did so well after Justin. The fear of being discovered, it...'

'You set up your friend.'

'He knew about it,' said Taylor. 'He ... he knew about it.'

'He found out?'

'He was ... he knew ... he told me to get help. He told me ... And I never did.'

Moorehead had been complicit, somehow. I knew that. All those murders, all corresponding with Taylor's visits, he had to have at least suspected something. So why did he never go to the police?

'So he knew? He knew and he didn't do anything?'

'He ... he was scared.'

'Why?'

Taylor had been expecting a beating. He'd been expecting more violence. Maybe he'd got used to the idea of it, become numb after the kicking that Burns's boys had handed him on the way over.

He hadn't been expecting someone to just sit there, ask him questions.

'Tell me, son.'

Taylor made a strange noise, a high-pitched, strangled sound that might have been the start of someone crying. But he shut it off quickly, and just closed his eyes.

Burns stood up. He said, 'I know this is tough. I know all you want to do is just run away. But I need to know, son. Do you understand that? I need to know the whole truth. And you and me we aren't leaving here until I'm satisfied.'

Taylor shuddered. His body bent at the waist, and he leaned forward as far as he could manage with the restraints. He started to make a low, moaning sound. His body trembled.

Burns walked behind Taylor, placed a hand lightly on the man's upper back. 'It's OK, son. It's OK. Let it all out.'

Standing on the sidelines, I was oddly removed from the scene. As though it wasn't really happening. I was merely observing. And as sick as it made me feel to watch, I couldn't simply walk out. Nor could I step in and interfere.

I looked at the two men standing beside me. I had never met them before, knew nothing about who they were at home, with their families, with their friends. I didn't know their personal beliefs or their ethical considerations. Did they have wives, children, mothers?

All I knew was, what I could see. Their stoic, unblinking reaction to the scene unfolding in front of them. It was as though they had simply turned themselves off, waiting for the next order from the big man himself.

'Oh, Jesus...'

'He can't help you now.'

Taylor lifted his eyes. He licked at his lips. 'Jesus saves...'

'What fuckin' eejit taught you that?'

And here, I always thought Burns was a good Christian.

'My mother ... my father.'

'Aye? And where are they now?'

'He killed himself.'

'Very fucking Christian. That come from having a pervert for a son?' He walked back around, sat in front of the man again. His gaze was steady. He had all the power. He always had the power.

Taylor didn't say anything.

'What's that, lad? Speak the fuck up! So your old man killed himself. And your mother?'

'I threw the bitch down the stairs.'

That one hit Burns. The ageing gangster sat back and looked at the pathetic wreck before him. 'A defenceless old woman?'

'Defenceless?' Taylor made a hacking sound that might have been laughter. 'She was tough as the Devil's own leather boots.'

'That right?'

'I was a boy, she taught me ... to fear.'

'Fear what?'

'My own fucking sin. You want to know about it? She'd hold me down while my father birched the fuck out of me. The pain. I remember the fucking pain. One lash for every sin I admitted to. And ten more when I lied.'

Burns didn't say anything.

'She could look at me, she could see my sins. She was a woman of God, you know that? A woman of fucking God and she'd been cursed with a deviant for a son. A deviant. No amount of birching or repentance could change that. Killing her, letting her die, it was a fucking mercy.'

The silence that followed was heavy, airless, stifling.

Burns stood up. He left the light and went to a canvas bag that had been dumped in one corner of the room. Took something from it and walked back to Taylor, sat in front of him again. He reached out with a plastic bottle of water in one hand. 'Here, son. Take a drink.'

Taylor straightened up. Burns undid the cap, held the bottle to Taylor's lips like one might a child. Taylor swallowed a few gulps before Burns took the water away again. 'Enough of the family truths, eh? Tell me about Alex Moorehead.'

Taylor took a deep breath. And talked. The story he told Burns was consistent with what I already knew, except for one major difference: Alex Moorehead had been in love with Jason.

And Jason had wanted to be in love with Alex. Except he couldn't. Because of his mother and father. Because of his own urges. The dark ones. The ones he truly felt ashamed of.

What attracted Taylor to Moorehead was the other man's innocence. Taylor thought that here was someone he could have a physical relationship with and not worry about what he was doing being wrong. They were both of age, although Taylor had known for a long time that innocence turned him on, and that his feelings about friends' younger brothers and even their children were inappropriate.

'You have to believe me that I never acted on those feelings. I buried them. Controlled them.'

And took them all out on Alex.

They never consummated any kind of relationship, but Taylor was always aware of how in thrall to him Moorehead was. Taylor was in control. He was always in control. Not just in the game-playing way, but in how close he let Alex get. Maybe that explained why Taylor had struck out on his own while Alex preferred to work for someone else; the man liked being told what to do. Maybe it explained why Moorehead had been a model prisoner, too: he had no issues with obeying instructions. In fact, he welcomed being told what to do. For a while.

'Alex was a natural submissive,' Taylor said. 'But everyone has their limits. I guess I found his.'

They argued. Moorehead wanted a real relationship. You can only remain in thrall to someone for so long, even when they think they know how to manipulate you. The fighting got worse.

'We were working late together, and I went to get a drink. He followed me into the kitchen, grabbed me, kissed me. I ... I wanted to. Maybe it could have worked, you know. But all the while, I could hear my mother's voice at the back of my mind. Calling me a sinner. Telling me that this was not God's will, that...' He shuddered.

They quit working together on the AV software that had been Taylor's pride and joy, based on the algorithms that Alex had developed.

'He told me I could keep the work, he'd wash his hands of it, didn't want to be reminded of me. When you lose control of someone, when they deny the power you held over them ... it makes you angry. You don't have the outlet for all those feelings...'

Listening to him, I felt this strange pressure building inside me. My ears threatened to pop, like I was on an aeroplane. I knew people who were into S&M relationships, had encountered my share of bondage disciples and power-play couples. For them it was a release, an equal relationship where the boundaries were defined and the power-play was shared. But what Taylor was describing sounded abusive, painting Alex Moorehead as a powerless and easily led dupe. I remembered talking to Elizabeth Farnham about her one night with Alex. 'He cried when we were done.'

Moorehead acted like a little boy.

Taylor was able to move all his desires on to the other man, create the kind of relationship he was looking for. And then it was all over. Before it could ever even begin.

He talked about the first time it happened, the first boy. He didn't name names, even though I knew who he was talking about. He talked about how he didn't intend anything to happen, that he suddenly realized what he was doing.

'I was disgusted. I know I'm sick. I know that it's wrong. But I could feel this need inside me. A fucking monster. A monster.'

He couldn't finish the act. Instead he killed the boy.

'It was like a release. Do you know what it felt like? It felt like I was saving him.'

One of the two men beside me turned and left the room. His movements were stiff, robotic. I felt like following him.

But I had to stay.

I had to see this through.

Burns said, 'So it wasn't about sex?'

'Yes ... no ... I don't know. I don't know.'

'How many more did you kill?'

'He was the first. I hid the body. Threw it in the water, hoped that he would sink, maybe be carried out to sea. His parents thought he'd run away. I didn't know what to do. Getting away with it, I wasn't relieved, I just felt this weight on my shoulders. My ... my parents and I never got on. There was no one I could turn to ... except Alex.'

That was when things got more complex. Taylor went to Alex. Reaching out for help. He didn't tell him that he'd killed a child, but he told him about his urges, how he had almost acted on them. Alex tried to help Taylor.

Taylor took advantage of the other man. Remembered all the ways in which he used to control him. Dangled the hope of there being some deeper connection between them to keep Moorehead on the hook. Like a drug addict or an alcoholic desperate to retain some connection to those around, to never truly be alone, he manipulated the other man completely.

Moorehead helped Taylor cover his tracks. He didn't always know what he was doing, but small favours here and there helped Taylor to continue doing what he did. For a while, he became convinced that he would be able to live with that other side of himself, that it was a vice like smoking or drinking, that it was something he simply couldn't deny. As long as he could control Alex, as long as the other man was there to dote after him, to remind him that he wasn't a monster, then everything was OK.

Moorehead was free from his mother and father. But the things they did to him never went away. He excised that violence on children, the same way they had to him. And sometimes he went too far.

But always, Alex was there to help him.

And then there was Justin Farnham.

When he started to talk about Justin, Taylor broke down again. He rocked in his chair, straining at the restraints. He started to grunt between gritted teeth.

It wasn't Burns he was looking to escape.

It was himself.

The enormity of what he'd done.

FORTY

'Alex never understood ... never wanted to understand ... He ... only did what I asked. Buried plastic bags and didn't look inside. Dropped boxes into dumps at night. Cleaned rooms top to bottom, never asking what happened. He ... he protected me. But ... never really knew what he was protecting me from.'

Another drink of water. Eager to talk, now. Someone was willing to listen. After all these years. His world had shrunk so that nothing existed outside of the harsh circle of light. There was no one else except David Burns, the man gently pressuring him to talk about things he had never found the courage to talk about before.

I was invisible. If he tried to look beyond the lights and into the darkness, he would see only shadows that he could dismiss as tricks of the mind.

He was broken. Ready to talk. In a strange way, I think he was grateful for what had happened to him that evening.

'Alex was supposed to be out on a job. I

waited until he had left the house and then went out for a walk through the fields. Feeling better than in a long time. Alex had bought me books he said helped him. He thought I was suffering from depression. I don't know what he thought that had to do with the things I made him do. But he was good at self-deception, same as me. Maybe more. The books helped a little, you know? Maybe he had a point.'

The books in his study. The ones he had never touched. They had helped. Or at least that's what he wanted to tell himself.

'There were groups online for people like me. Where I could talk to other people. Where we could share fantasies and ideas and they'd never have to be real. That was good. Healthier, you know, than acting on those impulses.'

Even now he was still justifying what he was. Making excuses.

'And then I saw him. He was heading home from playing with the other kids. He knew who I was, said I was a friend of Alex's. Offered to walk him home. All I wanted to do was walk beside him. I didn't ... I ... I thought, she's been dead for years. She doesn't have this power over me, you know?'

I tried to block out the next part of his story. Burns turned away from Taylor while he talked. He faced me, and I could see the look on his face that told me how hard it was for him to keep his instincts in check.

Burns was a man who believed in exercising control. He was determined to find the truth. He wanted a full confession.

And only then would he pass his full judgement.

'Tell me about Alex.'

'He was supposed to be home late. But he was early. Saw Justin's body. Knew what I had done. I told him it was an accident. He asked how many other accidents I'd had, what it was he'd really been doing for me over the years. I ... I told him the truth.'

The truth was what finished Moorehead. The truth was what made him realize his own complicity, made him just as guilty in his own mind as Taylor. Moorehead had allowed himself to be controlled by a domineering force in his life. A man who, like his father, had bullied and threatened him into behaving a certain way. A man who had violently gained power over Alex. Power that Alex had accepted unquestioningly.

But seeing the truth about Taylor, discovering the other man's dark secret and being unable to escape it, had tipped Moorehead over the edge. He had crumbled, broken down. And finally tumbled into a dark depression that made him feel he had to somehow pay for his own complicity.

'When he was done screaming and yelling and panicking ... he was somehow more submissive than I'd ever known. Like he was waiting for someone to tell him what to do. Like he'd been emptied inside. He needed to be filled up. With something. Anything.'

'So you told him to take the fall for you?'

'No. I told him to hide the body. I never expected ... When he played at finding the body again when he was helping the police, I thought ... I'm fucked. That's what I thought. When I saw it on the news, I expected the police to be at my door, handcuffs at the ready. But they never came.'

'And Alex took the blame. When he realized he couldn't tell them the truth about you.'

'I guess he was ... he ... in his head ... he was as guilty as me.'

And unspoken, there was that strange devotion. Alex Moorehead had loved Jason Taylor in his own fucked-up kind of way. And then he'd been betrayed. Completely. I could only imagine how that had felt. I could only image the kind of guilt he felt when he began to realize the extent of the other man's crimes.

If I can fall so hard for him, does that mean that I'm the same? That I deserve his punishment?

Taylor was calm, now. The sobbing was done. All he had left was the ability to keep talking. To explain everything that had happened. He sounded empty. Talking about all of this was an effort and a kind of release. As though Burns was his priest, his father confessor, capable of absolving him of all sins if only Taylor could admit to them.

I began to understand. To see the full picture.

When Taylor realized what was happening, he saw an opportunity to start his life again. Alex Moorehead was too fucked up and too afraid of Taylor to implicate the other man, so Taylor set up Moorehead's PC to look like he had spent years downloading child pornography. Combined with the murder of Justin Farnham, there would be no doubt in anyone's mind that Moorehead was a predator. And then, just to make sure we wouldn't be too stupid to find it, he offered his assistance to the investigating officers. Practically handed us the evidence.

And we were so appalled by the nature of the crime that we took it on face value.

We'd been duped. Suckered. Fucked over.

I wanted to break the spell of the moment, to walk over the artificial barrier created by the floodlights, haul the sick shitebag out of his chair and beat him half to death. Maybe all the way.

He'd destroyed so many innocent lives.

Not just the children. Alex Moorehead, too.

Moorehead's father had been a big force in his son's life. Alex had spent most of his life running from his father like he was the bogey-man. He loved and feared him at the same time. We'd discovered all of this in our initial investigation, and maybe that was why it had made sense to Wemyss that Alex would kill himself after talking to his father.

But I wondered if there was more than that.

If there was something else.

Moorehead's father had been missing since their little chat at the prison. He'd left without saying a word to the investigating officers.

Burns said, 'That's it, then?'

'Aye.'

'That's everything?'

'Aye.'

'No,' I said, and stepped forward. Blinking as I entered the light. 'That's not everything, is it?'

Taylor started to wriggle in his chair. The agitation that had affected him before returning.

Burns glared. I didn't give a shite.

'Alex told someone the truth. Before he killed himself. He was finally able to unburden his secrets to the one person who scared him more than you.'

Taylor turned his head away. 'No. No. No. No.'

I moved in. Didn't bother with the chair. Half-expected Burns to grab me, pull me back, assert his authority. But he did nothing of the sort. He merely stood back. A good-cop–bad-cop rhythm neither of us had prepared for.

I grabbed Taylor's face, wrenched his head round so that he was forced to look at me. 'He told someone. He told someone, and then they came to see you, didn't they?'

It made sense, now. The reason he attacked me. The reason he stopped himself short, as though suddenly scared to follow through.

I had thought he only killed children. I wasn't quite right.

'You killed him, didn't you? Jonathan Moorehead? A man grieving for a son he'd lost six years ago thanks to your fucked-up bullshit?'

Taylor started to weep. He shuddered and juddered and he wrenched his face from my grip and howled.

It made sense.

'Where's the body?'

'No.'

'Tell me.'

'No.'

'He was the first adult you killed. And when I came round, and you knew that I'd found you out, you thought you could do it again. But it wasn't the same. Jonathan Moorehead was an old man. He had been big once, but now he was old and frail. Past his prime. And you killed him easy. He didn't fight back. Or at least not hard enough.'

Taylor wept and rocked.

I stood up. 'Fuck it.'

Taylor howled.

Burns stepped forward as I left the light. Sat down in front of Taylor and calmed him. Gentle. The way someone might speak to a child. 'It's over now,' he said. 'You don't have to live with the guilt any more. Because you've admitted the truth, son. You've told the truth at last.'

Taylor calmed. Slowly.

Burns stood up and walked behind him, undid the restraints.

Then he came back round. Handed Taylor a pad of paper and a pen. 'The mothers of the boys you killed, all they want is peace of mind. They just need to know where their sons are buried. You think you can tell us? Names, dates, locations. That's all I want. That's all they want.'

'What happens then?'

'I set you free.'

Taylor's eyes widened. He sniffed back snot and blood. 'Free?'

'No concern of mine, then, son. All I want is to give these women peace of mind.'

'Free?'

Burns nodded. He seemed sincere. Calm and rational.

Taylor wrote.

No one moved. No one said anything. The only sound came from the scribble of the pen-nib on the paper.

When he was done, he handed the paper back to Burns. 'I'm thirsty.'

Burns nodded. He took the paper, handed Taylor what was left of the plastic bottle. Walked out of the light, handed the pad to one of the men standing beside me.

Taylor gulped at the water.

Burns turned, walked back into the light and in front of Taylor. He slammed his open palm against the bottom of the bottle, slammed it into Taylor's mouth. The other man made a strange noise and fell back, taking the chair with him. He spat out the bottle with a spray of bloodied liquid.

Burns was old, but still as dangerous and violent as he had ever been. He laid into Taylor with ferocity. Delivered kicks to the kidneys, hauled the other man up on to his feet and savagely slammed hard, bony fists into his face.

Taylor collapsed.

Burns stood over him. Kicked the poor bastard over and over again. In the body, in the face. Finally, he stomped down hard on the man's skull. Once. Twice. Three times.

When it was over, he stepped back. Nodded to one of the thugs. The man stepped forward, moved behind Taylor and pulled him to his feet. Then he produced a knife.

He held Taylor like a pig, hauling back the man's head by pulling on his hair. Then he slit Taylor's throat. A practised motion, made me think he had abattoir experience. Or worse.

I thought about Charles Leigh, the man who had made this the Murder House.

Taylor slid to the ground. Gasped, bubbled and shook.

And finally, he was still.

FORTY-ONE

That was the test.

Right there. Everything else was a tease, a lead-up.

Burns wanted to know if I was still a straight-up citizen. Testing my sense of justice.

Was I playing a part?

Or had I really allowed him to do what he did because I thought that Jason Taylor deserved what he got?

Tough to say. Tough to know.

Back at the office, I called Griggs on his unlisted mobile. Went straight to voicemail.

'It's done,' I said.

Jason Taylor hit the headlines.

The tabloids had a field day.

Redboot quietly shut up shop. Its servers went dead. Its clients found new tech geeks. Two days after the offices closed for good someone set a fire on the ground floor. No one was hurt, thank goodness.

The police investigation found no leads.

Taylor was seen at various places up and

down the country for at least six months. Every sighting was a dead end. He became a bogey-man and whenever the media ran down their top scumbags, he was somewhere on the list.

But only six people knew the truth.

Myself.

Burns.

His thugs.

Griggs.

And Susan.

My business account was credited with £12,000 from Burns Holdings, Inc. The Big Man told me that it was best to pay 'little and often' to avoid difficult questions. He said there would be more work for me if I was interested. 'But nothing that would offend your delicate sensibilities.' I told him I'd consider what he had to say.

We danced. I followed the steps expected of me.

Kellen came to see me three days after Taylor vanished.

We talked in my office.

She remained standing throughout. Had the kind of pent-up energy you see in caged lions.

'They shut it down. The investigation.'

'Can I ask why?'

'Lack of compelling evidence.' She shook

her head. 'They opened it. They handed it to me on a plate and now they take it away.'

'That's life.'

'Anyone ever told you that you're a lucky man, McNee?'

I shook my head.

It was the truth.

'Lucky' was the last word I'd use.

As she left, she said, 'I'll be watching.'

'You're keeping the file open?'

'I'm a good cop. I do as I'm told.'

'But off the book?'

'Like a fucking hawk.'

They found Jonathan Moorehead in a shallow grave about two hundred yards from Taylor's house. He had been bludgeoned to death. The object used was round, heavy and probably some kind of ornament. Taylor had disposed of it.

Probably in the ocean.

I phoned Wemyss, gave him my pet theory regarding what happened in the interview and what happened afterward. I made it sound like pure speculation, but Taylor had given me enough that I knew it was true.

'Fits with what we know,' Wemyss said. 'Jesus fucking Christ, I hope we find him.'

I didn't say anything.

Wemyss added, 'I hope the twisted cunt gets what he deserves.'

FORTY-TWO

Susan met me at the lay-by.

I knew we were safe to meet out here. No one was watching. No one would think to look here.

This was where everything had begun. Where I'd had the accident that led to my leaving the force. Where I'd started the journey to become a person I never expected to be.

'How are you, Steed?'

'Good as you might expect,' I said.

'You never told Griggs how you got in close with Burns. What it was you did.'

'Found common ground,' I said.

She nodded. 'He's keeping you on the fringe for now?'

'He's not an idiot.'

'We'll do our best to protect you.'

'From Burns? Or from the law?'

She didn't say anything.

'If it was up to me, I'd ask you to kill him.'

'What would happen if he did die?'

'No one would cry.'

I nodded.

'But then we'd be no better than him, right?'

'Right.'

She said, 'I'm sorry. About us, I mean.'

'It couldn't work. Too much history.'

'Sandy's a good man.'

'I'm sure he is.'

I handed her the envelope. We were keeping everything old school. Paper trails. No electronic communication. Nothing that could be traced without our knowledge.

Our fingers touched.

She hesitated. Kissed me quickly on the lips.

Neither of us said anything.

She went to her car, drove away.

I stayed. Watched the sunset.

Thought about the dead.

NOTES AND ACKNOWLEDGEMENTS

This is the fourth McNee novel. But I hope it's not been too hard to catch up if you're new to the dour Dundonian Detective. It was also the last to be completed in Dundee, a city that has been very kind to me over the last fifteen years. It will not be the last book to be set there, however.

As usual, it's worth pointing out that while Dundee is a very real place, the situations, people and even a few of the places mentioned are fictional. A few real life names have snuck in, and anywhere you think you recognize is probably not the scene of the crime. Like the Phoenix Bar – still one of my favourite pubs, and I hope that having everyone drink in there has made up for the decorational faux-pas of one of my previous novels. If you think you've found a mistake in local geography or history, then it's likely to have been for reasons of artistic licence. But even if it's not, then I hope you still enjoy the story. That's the important thing.

No novel is written alone by any author, so

here are a few people who helped along the road to getting this book out there. Whatever you like in here is probably thanks to them.

Dot and Martin McLean – who instilled in their son a love of words, books and story-telling. And wine. With this fourth book, he has now made enough to buy you a postcard of a house in France...

Allan Guthrie – Top Secret (literary) Agent and Top Secret Weapon at the Literary Death Match...

Kate Lyall Grant – whose support and enthusiasm for the novel has been absolutely brilliant; a pleasure to be working with you.

Anna Telfer – and the copy-editing team at Severn House, who did a great job making me question certain parts of the manuscript that didn't add up. Your patience and rigour is massively appreciated. Any writer who claims not to need an editor is deluded.

Ross Bradshaw – whose hard work at Five Leaves has helped the McNee series to keep on going. Thank you for all your support and for taking a chance on a debut novel all those years ago. And for anyone reading this, if you're ever in Nottingham, you really do need to visit the Five Leaves Bookstore.

331

Robert Simon Macduff-Duncan – pedant-in-chief, the man with all the answers and expert at getting oversized bookcases through undersized doorways. Anything that's legally accurate in the process of Scots law is down to him. Anything that's wrong is because I didn't listen to him (or ask the right questions).

Mark Wade – without whom, Wemyss would be simply The Fat Cop With No Name.

Booksellers, librarians and readers around the world – you know who you are and you are amazing. Even the ones who don't like naughty words.

Lesley McDowell – for far too many good reasons (and far too many glasses of wine). And Moriarty. How could I forget Moriarty?

The usual suspects – to list you all would take a whole other book, but you know who you are and you know why you're important...

In memory of Peter Heims (1929–2013) – who so very kindly and patiently answered questions about the life of an investigator when I first embarked on writing a novel about a British PI.